SAMUEL JOHNSON
IS INDIGNANT

ALSO BY LYDIA DAVIS

NOVEL

The End of the Story (1995)

STORIES

The Thirteenth Woman and Other Stories (1976)

Sketches for a Life of Wassilly (1981)

Story and Other Stories (1983)

Break It Down (1986)

Almost No Memory (1997)

SELECTED TRANSLATIONS

Death Sentence by Maurice Blanchot (1978)

The Madness of the Day by Maurice Blanchot (1981)

The Last Man by Maurice Blanchot (1987)

Scratches by Michel Leiris (1991)

Hélène by Pierre Jean Jouve (1993)

Scraps by Michel Leiris (1997)

By Way of Swann's by Marcel Proust (2002)

SAMUEL JOHNSON IS INDIGNANT

STORIES

LYDIA DAVIS

Picador

Farrar, Straus and Giroux
New York

www.picadorusa.com

Picador® is a U.S. registered trademark and is used by Farrar, Straus and Giroux under license from Pan Books Limited.

For information on Picador Reading Group Guides, as well as ordering, please contact the Trade Marketing department at St. Martin's Press.
Phone: 1-800-221-7945 extension 763
Fax: 212-677-7456
E-mail: trademarketing@stmartins.com

Library of Congress Cataloging-in-Publication Data

Davis, Lydia.
Samuel Johnson is indignant : stories / Lydia Davis.—1st Picador ed.

    p. cm.
   ISBN 0-312-42056-0
   1. United States—Social life and customs—20th century—Fiction.
I. Title.

PS3554.A9356 S36 2002
813'.54—dc21   2002066775

First published by McSweeney's Books, New York

D 10 9 8 7 6 5

For Alan, Theo, and Daniel

Grateful acknowledgment to the editors of the following magazines in which these stories first appeared, sometimes in a slightly different form: *American Letters & Commentary*: "How Difficult" and "Selfish"; *Bomb*: "First Grade: Handwriting Practice," "A Double Negative," "The Old Dictionary," "They Take Turns Using a Word They Like," "Special," "Spring Spleen," "Working Men," "Young and Poor," and "Almost Over: Separate Bedrooms"; *Conjunctions*: "Happy Memories"; *Dyslexia*: "My Husband and I"; *Fourteen Hills*: "New Year's Resolution"; *Granta*: "The Furnace"; *Hambone*: "Betrayal," "Right and Wrong," "Interesting," and "Company"; *Hayden's Ferry Review*: "Boring Friends" and "City People; *Hodos*: "Companion"; *Insurance*: "Special Chair," "Samuel Johnson Is Indignant," and "Examples of *Remember*"; *Joe*: "The Meeting"; *Metro Times*: "Our Trip"; *The New Yorker*: "Thyroid Diary"; *Noon*: "Certain Knowledge from Herodotus," "Honoring the Subjunctive," "Information from the North Concerning the Ice," "Away from Home," and "Acknowledgment"; *The Partisan Review*: "Old Mother and the Grouch"; *Salt Hill Journal*: "Finances"; *Shiny*: "Money" and "Jury Duty"; *Sulfur*: "Priority" and "Her Damage"; *Timothy McSweeney's Quarterly*: "A Mown Lawn," "Marie Curie, So Honorable Woman," and "Oral History (with Hiccups)"; *Tin House*: "Letter to a Funeral Parlor"

"Alvin the Typesetter" first appeared in the anthology *Here Lies* (ed. David Gilbert and Karl Roeseler; Trip Street Press: San Francisco, 2001); "Blind Date" first appeared as a limited-edition chapbook from Chax Press, Tucson, in 1999.

"The Old Dictionary" also appeared in *Harper's* magazine and was included in the anthology *Mother Reader: Essential Writings on Motherhood* (ed. Moyra Davey; Seven Stories Press: New York, 2001)

"The White Tribe," "Mir the Hessian," "In a Northern Country," "The Patient," "The Transformation," "Murder in Bohemia," "The Silence of Mrs. Iln," and "My Neighbors in a Foreign Place" were first published in *The Thirteenth Woman and Other Stories* (Living Hand Editions: New York, 1976).

"Betrayal" also appeared in *Best American Poetry 1999* (ed. Robert Bly; Scribner: New York, 1999) and "A Mown Lawn" also appeared in *Best American Poetry 2001* (ed. Robert Hass; Scribner: New York, 2001).

Support during the period in which many of these stories were written was given by three organizations to which I am very grateful: the John Simon Guggenheim Memorial Foundation, the Lila Wallace-Reader's Digest Fund, and the Lannan Foundation. — L.D.

CONTENTS

SAMUEL JOHNSON
IS INDIGNANT

BORING FRIENDS

We know only four boring people. The rest of our friends we find very interesting. However, most of the friends we find interesting find us boring: the most interesting find us the most boring. The few who are somewhere in the middle, with whom there is reciprocal interest, we distrust: at any moment, we feel, they may become too interesting for us, or we too interesting for them.

A MOWN LAWN

She hated a *mown lawn*. Maybe that was because *mow* was the reverse of *wom*, the beginning of the name of what she was— a *woman*. A *mown lawn* had a sad sound to it, like a *long moan*. From her, a *mown lawn* made a *long moan*. *Lawn* had some of the letters of *man*, though the reverse of *man* would be *Nam*, a bad war. A *raw war*. *Lawn* also contained the letters of *law*. In fact, *lawn* was a contraction of *lawman*. Certainly a *lawman* could and did *mow* a *lawn*. *Law and order* could be seen as starting from *lawn order*, valued by so many Americans. *More lawn* could be made using a *lawn mower*. A *lawn mower* did make *more lawn*. *More lawn* was a contraction of *more lawmen*. Did *more lawn* in America make *more lawmen* in America? Did *more lawn* make *more Nam*? *More mown lawn* made *more long moan*, from her. Or a *lawn mourn*. So often, she said, Americans wanted *more mown lawn*. All of America might be one *long mown lawn*. A *lawn* not *mown* grows *long*, she said: better a *long lawn*. Better a *long lawn* and a *mole*. Let the *lawman* have the *mown lawn*, she said. Or the *moron*, the *lawn moron*.

CITY PEOPLE

They have moved to the country. The country is nice enough: there are quail sitting in the bushes and frogs peeping in the swamps. But they are uneasy. They quarrel more often. They cry, or she cries and he bows his head. He is pale all the time now. She wakes in a panic at night, hearing him sniffle. She wakes in a panic again, hearing a car go up the driveway. In the morning there is sunlight on their faces but mice are chattering in the walls. He hates the mice. The pump breaks. They replace the pump. They poison the mice. Their neighbor's dog barks. It barks and barks. She could poison the dog.

"We're city people," he says, "and there aren't any nice cities to live in."

BETRAYAL

In her fantasies about other men, as she grew older, about men other than her husband, she no longer dreamed of sexual intimacy, as she once had, perhaps for revenge, when she was angry, perhaps out of loneliness, when he was angry, but only of an affection and a profound sort of understanding, a holding of hands and a gazing into eyes, often in a public place like a café. She did not know if this change came out of respect for her husband, for she did truly respect him, or out of plain weariness, at the end of the day, or out of a sense of what activity she could expect from herself, even in a fantasy, now that she was a certain age. And when she was particularly tired, she couldn't even manage the affection and the profound understanding, but only the mildest sort of companionship, such as being in the same room alone together, sitting in chairs. And it happened that as she grew older still, and more tired, and then still older, and still more tired, another change occurred and she found that even the mildest sort of companionship, alone together, was now too vigorous to sustain, and her fantasies were limited to a

4

calm sort of friendliness among other friends, the sort she really could have had with any man, with a clear conscience, and did in fact have with many, who were friends of her husband's too, or not, a friendliness that gave her comfort and strength, at night, when the friendships in her waking life were not enough, or had not been enough by the end of the day. And so these fantasies came to be indistinguishable from the reality of her waking life, and should not have been any sort of betrayal at all. Yet because they were fantasies she had alone, at night, they continued to feel like some sort of betrayal, and perhaps, because approached in this spirit of betrayal, as perhaps they had to be, to be any comfort and strength, continued to be, in fact, a sort of betrayal.

THE WHITE TRIBE

We live near a tribe of bloodless white people. Day and night they come to steal things from us. We have put up tall wire fences but they spring over them like gazelles and grin fiendishly up at us where we stand looking out of our windows. They rub the tops of their heads until their thin flaxen hair stands up in tufts, and they strut back and forth over our gravel terrace. While we are watching this performance, others among them have crept into our garden and are furtively taking our roses, stuffing them into bags which hang from their naked shoulders. They are pitifully thin, and as we watch them we become ashamed of our fence. Yet when they go, slipping away like white shadows in the gloom, we grow angry at the devastation they have left among our Heidelbergs and Lady Belpers, and resolve to take more extreme measures against them. It is not always the roses they come for, but sometimes—though the countryside for miles is covered with boulders and shards of stone—they carry away the very rocks from our woods, and walking out in the morning we find the ground pitted with hollows where pale bugs squirm blindly down into the earth.

OUR TRIP

My mother asks on the phone how our drive home was, and I say "Fine," which is not the truth but a fiction. You can't tell everyone the truth all the time, and you certainly can't tell anyone the whole truth, ever, because it would take too long.

The word "fine" is the greatest abbreviation and obviously wrong. Even a long drive with two people can be difficult, and with three it can be much worse. We almost always start a trip with some cross words anyway, because I can't seem to leave on time and Mac can't stand leaving a minute late, and then there's Junior. Mac generally cheers up once we're on our way, but this time he went on snapping at me because I didn't tell him where to turn far enough ahead of time or I gave him too many instructions at once. On top of that I kept telling him to shift up. The car is old and the transmission is noisy, so it's hard for me to tell if Mac's in the right gear.

Then we began to smell burning oil. There was another van in front of us, packed full of some religious group, so we knew it could be them, and when we came to a garage they pulled in and that was the end of the burning smell, so Mac's mood improved a little.

But we were still in mountain country, and Junior started saying which mountains he was planning to climb next year—I'm going to climb that one, he said, pointing, and that one, what's the name of that one? Whiteface? I'm going to climb Whiteface, and then that one. I'm going to climb that one over there, what's the name of that one? Charles? What about that one over there? What's the name? Mungus? Fungus? Mangoes? Mongoose? Hey, look at that one—that's gotta be the biggest one. What's the name of that one?

I was turning the map this way and that, trying to figure out what the names of these mountains were, and even though Junior was talking so fast, and acting more like six years old than nine, I didn't see any big harm in this conversation. But Mac said he felt as if he was on a tour bus and would we be quiet. Anything a little out of control makes him nervous.

Eventually we got onto the highway and then of course I had to go to the bathroom. I always have to go to the bathroom when we get onto a major highway. Luckily we came to a rest stop pretty soon, and since we were there anyway we sat down at a picnic table to eat our sandwiches. The picnic table wasn't all that clean—it had a few sticky spills and some bird lime on it—but the sun was warm and I was just beginning to relax and enjoy watching the people walk past us to the restrooms when Junior came back from the restrooms and asked me for money for a soda. He always asks for a soda if he sees a soda machine, and I usually say No, which is what I said this time.

Now he decided to make an issue of it, and said he wouldn't get back in the car if we didn't get him a soda, and he went off over the grass toward the Dog Walk Area and sat down to sulk on some kind of large bent pipe sticking up out of the grass. So then Mac, who is more likely to give in than I am, said to let him have his soda, and I called Junior back and gave him the money and he went off and came back with the soda. I made the mistake of reading the ingredients, though, and when I saw how much caffeine there was in it, I began going on about that and I wouldn't stop, even back in the car, until I saw that now Junior was getting upset again and the whole thing was pointless. So I shut up and started cleaning my hands with some pre-moistened towelettes called Wet Ones which have a sickly sweet smell to them, and the smell filled the car so badly that now the two of them turned on me.

After that, Junior was pretty cheerful because the soda made him feel a few years older, I could see it by the way he slouched with his knees apart and his hands dangling, and the atmosphere in the car improved even more when a crowd of men and women on motorcycles passed us going about 90 miles per hour. Mac said he hoped they would get stopped for speeding, and the thought of that cheered him up so much he started a conversation with me. He asked me what kind of car we should get when we bought a new car. He pointed out a Dodge Caravan, and Junior woke up from his daydream and said he wanted a Corvette. Mac asked where he was going to get the $30,000. Junior didn't have an answer, then he thought to ask how much Mac had paid for our Voyager. $7,000, Mac said, which stumped Junior but didn't seem fair to me, because he didn't tell Junior he had gotten it second-hand, so I threw in that information just to make it fair, and of course Junior said he would get his Corvette second-hand too. Cars aren't my favorite subject, though, so pretty soon we had run it into the ground and I went back to doing what I had been doing, which was looking out the window.

We passed a spot where the Highway Department had cleared the forest by the side of the road and planted some trees. The trees were covered with shriveled reddish foliage and obviously dying. This started me thinking about deforestation, and then about the disappearance of family farms, which somehow took me back to caffeine levels again. At that point, I started trying to identify the new trees I had learned on our vacation, and when I gave up on that I just watched the fat on my arm ripple in the wind from the open window.

Things went on pretty much like that. At some point I began to think I had spider bites on my legs; later Mac asked me if I had put something strange in the sandwiches; Junior rolled up the toll ticket to make a telescope, and Mac yelled at him; but then we all quieted down to watch the remains of a pretty dramatic accident by the side of the road.

At the rest stop I had been thinking that about 50 percent of the people I saw looked as though they'd had a better vacation than we had. But then 50 percent of them looked as though they'd had a worse one, so I felt alright about it.

When we were twenty minutes from home, Junior

wanted to stop at a Holiday Inn and spend the night and couldn't understand why we said no. But I realized about then that as a family we have a certain kind of loyalty to each other, and the way it works is that no two of us will get mad at the third one at the same time, except occasionally, as in the case of the Wet Ones.

SPECIAL CHAIR

He and I are both teachers in the university system and we
will be teachers until we are too old to teach, and we would
certainly like to be given a special chair at our universities,
but what we have gotten so far is the wrong kind of special
chair, a special chair belonging to a friend, a chair that
swivels and has splayed feet and is special to her for reasons
we can't remember. We who teach in the university system
would like a special chair so that we would be paid more and
not have to teach as much and not have to sit on so many
committees—we would sit instead on our special chair. But
we have not been given any special chairs by our universities,
only this strange heavy chair belonging to our friend, who
moved away many years ago and had to leave it behind, and
who does not want to give it up for reasons we have forgotten or never knew. All this time we have been employed by
our universities only to teach from year to year without even
the security of tenure. But now one of us has had some good
luck and has been given a job with tenure, though not by his
own university, and in leaving his present job, the job with-

out tenure, he must also leave behind the chair special to our friend, because he is moving far away and there will not be room for it where he is going. Even though there is a great deal of large empty space in the state where he is going, more empty space than practically any other state but Wyoming, he will be living there in a very small house, too small for an extra chair, especially such a heavy one made out of a wine barrel. And so I will be the one to keep our friend's chair for her now; it has passed from him to me, though not without effort, since it is so heavy. And perhaps, I am thinking, her special chair with its strange red vinyl upholstery, with its bunghole in the back, and its genuine cork, will now bring me good luck of a professional kind too.

CERTAIN KNOWLEDGE
FROM HERODOTUS

These are the facts about the fish in the Nile:

PRIORITY

It should be so simple. You do what you can while he is awake, and then once he is asleep, you do what you can only do when he is asleep, beginning with the most important thing. But it is not so simple.

You ask yourself what is the most important thing. It should be easy to say which thing has priority and go and do it. But not just one thing has priority, and not just two or three. When several things have priority, which of the several things having priority is given priority?

In the time in which you can do something, the time when he is asleep, you can write a letter that has to be written immediately because many things depend on it. And yet if you write the letter, your plants will not get watered and it is a very hot day. You have already put them out on the balcony hoping the rain will water them, but this summer it almost never rains. You have already taken them in from the balcony hoping that if they are out of the wind they will not have to be watered as often, but they will still have to be watered.

And yet if you water the plants, you will not write the letter, on which so much depends. You will also not tidy the kitchen and living room, and later you will become confused and cross because of the disorder. One counter is covered with shopping lists and pieces of glassware your husband bought at a liquidation sale. It should be simple enough to put the glassware away, but you can't put it away until you wash it, you can't wash it until the sink is clear of dirty dishes, and you can't wash the dishes until you empty the drainboard. If you begin by emptying the drainboard, you may not get any farther, while he is asleep, than washing the dishes.

You may decide that the plants have priority, in the end, because they are alive. Then you may decide, since you must find a way of organizing your priorities, that all the living things in the house will have priority, starting with the youngest and smallest human being. That should be clear enough. But then, though you know exactly how to care for the mouse, the cat, and the plants, you are not sure how to give priority to the baby, the older boy, yourself, and your husband. It is certainly true that the larger and older the living thing is, the harder it is to know how to care for it.

THE MEETING

I tried so hard, the clothes I wore, new look I had, I thought.
Competent, I thought, casual. New raincoat. Brown.
Things seemed all right at first, promising, in the waiting
room. Top secretary offered me the comfortable chair, a cup
of tea—top secretary or second secretary. Declined the tea—
how could I swallow it, how could I even hold the cup?
Opened my little book. Thought once I got in there he
might even ask me what I was reading—Wait, he might
say, is that Addison? Kept my head down, eyes on the page.
Listened to the secretaries, thought I was learning the inside
dope. Feeling smart. Thought I was all buttoned up. Yes,
and now here we were alone for the first time, at last, and I
thought we might have a special rapport, he might become
a friend, at least. I thought he might say to himself: Here is
this woman, this attractive woman, I've talked to her before,
never at length, unfortunately, now she's here across my
desk from me in an attractive raincoat with some jewelry on.
I thought he might say: She's quiet but I know from what
I've heard and from the way she sits there so composed,

holding that small book bound in green leather—could it be Addison?—that she's intelligent, though obviously shy, it will be interesting to talk to her... Here he is, the boss, and there are no distractions, there's no one coming into the room, no one offering something from a tray, no one walking past, no one drinking next to him, no one asking him a sudden question that left me out, rudely, no one standing in a circle with him, here we are alone, my face floating over that piled desk. But he!—he rails against the whole project, he uses bad language, though it isn't my fault, it really isn't my fault, what he doesn't like, the change of title, and in fact he's wrong about that, things have to change, even titles have to change. How he jumps on me, how he strafes me, how he slangs me. I'm rocked. Of course—anyone can make an appointment to see the President, that's the easy part. I try again, surface and take another breath, say something, he stops railing and listens, he says something back, asks me a decent question, but I can't remember that name, I just can't remember it, me with my shaky voice, now what can I say, don't have a single million-dollar word, say something dumb, now he's doing his best, he's trying to remember his manners. But after all that yelling he says he isn't the one who can help me, no, even though they said I should go talk to him myself, they both said that. And they know him, I thought I could trust them, just plant the idea in his head at least, they said. I guess maybe they sold me a pup. What a blunder. And I wore all this jewelry, every piece I had that was decent. He never noticed, I'm sure. No, he just said to himself: Not my concern, sorry. Wait, I thought, give me time, another five minutes. But it's no use, now he stands up and sticks his hand across the desk at an angle and flat as a piece of cardboard, he's offering to shake, it's his signal, I'm supposed to leave. Well, lost opportunity, Mr. President! Old bean! We're not all so clever, you know—not on the spot like that. Beanpole! Some day you'll make me an offer, I'll say I can't help you. Such a mistake, even to go in there. So wrong. Some other frequency. Can't do anything right. Not worth shucks. Strange hat, brown coat, drooping hem, bare neck, yellow skin, wrong jewelry, too much jewelry. So many mistakes. Electric hair. So many mistakes. Too much, too little, wrong time, wrong place, can't do it right. Do it anyway. Spoil it. Do it again. Spoil it again. A slime, a weed. I wanted respect. Did he even see me? Did he even see my head poking up above those piles? He was seeing another appointment! This was my appointment! Maybe the rain-coat gave a bad impression. Maybe I was wrong to wear brown. Maybe he thought: Uh-oh, there's something depressing out there in the waiting room. Brown woman with a proposal, sitting in a chair with her book. And then I wasn't prepared. Didn't know the name. I nodded. Anyone can nod. I didn't know what was coming! I was so dumb. I'm aching. What shame—ready to kill. Wish I'd had my mother with me. She would have said something. A gasbag. He would have said she was a gabby old woman, an ulcer— What's she doing in here? Who let her in? Get her out of here! In her pastel suit. But there she'd be. She'd account for him. She'd give it to him—right in the clock! He'd say: Get the old bag off my dark wood paneling! That's my mother! What a barney, hoo-ha! She'd give him a mouse, all right! He'd say: Get the old bag in her pink suit away from in

front of my dark wood paneling! Get him, mother! Sic him!
Old Iowa bag. Come in here with her replaced hip, her
replaced knee, one leg shorter than the other, built-up shoe.
Determined. She'd lam him in his little Mary, quick and
smart, she'd have the edge on him. What's this? he would
have said. Kick this old lady out of here! In her spring suit.
He might have used bad language about her too: Kick this
old fart out of here! Maybe I should have taken my whole
family in there with me. Brother watching, father watching,
sister getting up to help. But Mother's the one who would
floor him. Mother would thrash him, she'd baste his jacket.
She's high-rent. She would have said, Be nice to her! He
wasn't nice to me. That's *my daughter!* He wasn't nice. She
would have given him a piece of her fist. See this?—shaking
it right in his pan. Names for him. She doesn't come as a
water-carrier for anyone. Annihilate him, Mother! Crush
him! No more—Bam!—President of this place. New
President, please! Better one, please. Oh boy! Sock! You'll
see, Mr. President! Summer-complaint! Dog's breakfast!

COMPANION

We are sitting here together, my digestion and I. I am reading a book and it is working away at the lunch I ate a little while ago.

BLIND DATE

"There isn't really much to tell," she said, but she would tell it if I liked. We were sitting in a midtown luncheonette. "I've only had one blind date in my life. And I didn't really have it. I can think of more interesting situations that are like a blind date—say when someone gives you a book as a present, when they fix you up with that book. I was once given a book of essays about reading, writing, book collecting. I felt it was a perfect match. I started reading it right away, in the back seat of the car. I stopped listening to the conversation in the front. I like to read about how other people read and collect books, even how they shelve their books. But by the time I was done with the book, I had taken a strong dislike to the author's personality. I won't have another date with *her*!" She laughed. Here we were interrupted by the waiter, and then a series of incidents followed that kept us from resuming our conversation that day.

The next time the subject came up, we were sitting in two Adirondack chairs looking out over a lake in, in fact, the Adirondacks. We were content to sit in silence at first. We were tired. We had been to the Adirondack Museum that day and seen many things of interest, including old guide boats and good examples of the original Adirondack chair. Now we watched the water and the edge of the woods, each thinking, I was sure, about James Fenimore Cooper. After some parties of canoers had gone by, older people in canvas boating hats, their quiet voices carrying far over the water to us, we went on talking. These were precious days of holiday together, and we were finishing many unfinished conversations.

"I was fifteen or sixteen, I guess," she said. "I was home from boarding school. Maybe it was summer. I don't know where my parents were. They were often away. They often left me alone there, sometimes for the evening, sometimes for weeks at a time. The phone rang. It was a boy I didn't know. He said he was a friend of a boy from school—I can't remember who. We talked a little and then he asked me if I wanted to have dinner with him. He sounded nice enough so I said I would, and we agreed on a day and a time and I told him where I lived.

"But after I got off the phone, I began thinking, worrying. What had this other boy said about me? What had the two of them said about me? Maybe I had some kind of a reputation. Even now I can't imagine that what they said was completely pure or innocent—for instance, that I was pretty and fun to be with. There had to be something nasty about it, two boys talking privately about a girl. The awful word that began to occur to me was *fast*. She's *fast*. I wasn't actually very fast. I was faster than some but not as fast as others. The more I imagined the two boys talking about me the worse I felt.

"I liked boys. I liked the boys I knew in a way that was much more innocent than they probably thought. I trusted them more than girls. Girls hurt my feelings, girls ganged up on me. I always had boys who were my friends, starting back when I was nine and ten and eleven. I didn't like this feeling that two boys were talking about me.

"Well, when the day came, I didn't want to go out to dinner with this boy. I just didn't want the difficulty of this date. It scared me—not because there was anything scary about the boy but because he was a stranger, I didn't know him. I didn't want to sit there face to face in some restaurant and start from the very beginning, knowing nothing. It didn't feel right. And there was the burden of that recommendation—'Give her a try.'

"Then again, maybe there were other reasons. Maybe I had been alone in that apartment so much by then that I had retreated into some kind of inner, unsociable space that was hard to come out of. Maybe I felt I had disappeared and I was comfortable that way and did not want to be forced back into existence. I don't know.

"At six o'clock, the buzzer rang. The boy was there, downstairs. I didn't answer it. It rang again. Still I did not answer it. I don't know how many times it rang or how long he leaned on it. I let it ring. At some point, I walked the length of the living room to the balcony. The apartment was four stories up. Across the street and down a flight of stone steps was a park. From the balcony on a clear day you could look out over the park and see all the way across town, maybe a mile, to the other river. At this point I think I ducked down or got down on my hands and knees and

24

inched my way to the edge of the balcony. I think I looked over far enough to see him down there on the sidewalk below—looking up, as I remember it. Or he had gone across the street and was looking up. He didn't see me.

"I know that as I crouched there on the balcony or just back from it I had some impression of him being puzzled, disconcerted, disappointed, at a loss what to do now, not prepared for this—prepared for all sorts of other ways the date might go, other difficulties, but not for no date at all. Maybe he also felt angry or insulted, if it occurred to him then or later that maybe he hadn't made a mistake but that I had deliberately stood him up, and not the way I did it— alone up there in the apartment, uncomfortable and embarrassed, chickening out, hiding out—but, he would imagine, in collusion with someone else, a girlfriend or boyfriend, confiding in them, snickering over him.

"I don't know if he called me, or if I answered the phone if it rang. I could have given some excuse—I could have said I had gotten sick or had to go out suddenly. Or maybe I hung up when I heard his voice. In those days I did a lot of avoiding that I don't do now—avoiding confrontations, avoiding difficult encounters. And I did a fair amount of lying that I also don't do now.

"What was strange was how awful this felt. I was treating a person like a thing. And I was betraying not just him but something larger, some social contract. When you knew a decent person was waiting downstairs, someone you had made an appointment with, you did not just not answer the buzzer. What was even more surprising to me was what I felt about myself in that instant. I was behaving as though

I had no responsibility to anyone or anything, and that made me feel as though I existed outside society, some kind of criminal, or didn't exist at all. I was annihilating myself even more than him. It was an awful violation."

She paused, thoughtful. We were sitting inside now, because it was raining. We had come inside to sit in a sort of lounge or recreation room provided for guests of that lakeside camp. The rain fell every afternoon there, sometimes for minutes, sometimes for hours. Across the water, the white pines and spruces were very still against the gray sky. The water was silver. We did not see any of the water birds we sometimes saw paddling around the edges of the lake—teals and loons. Inside, a fire burned in the fireplace. Over our heads hung a chandelier made of antlers. Between us stood a table constructed of a rough slab of wood resting on the legs of a deer, complete with hooves. On the table stood a lamp made from an old gun. She looked away from the lake and around the room. "In that book about the Adirondacks I was reading last night," she remarked, "he says this was what the Adirondacks was all about, I mean the Adirondacks style: things made from things."

A month or so later, when I was home again and she was back in the city, we were talking on the telephone and she said she had been hunting through one of the old diaries she had on her shelf there, that might say exactly what had happened—though of course, she said, she would just be filling in the details of something that did not actually happen. But she couldn't find this incident written down anywhere, which of course made her wonder if she had gotten the dates really wrong and she wasn't even in boarding school anymore by then. Maybe she was in college by then. But she decided to believe what she had told me. "But I'd forgotten how much I wrote about boys," she added. "Boys and books. What I wanted more than anything else at the age of sixteen was a great library."

EXAMPLES OF *REMEMBER*

Remember that thou art but dust.
I shall try to *bear it in mind*.

OLD MOTHER
AND THE GROUCH

"Meet the sourpuss," says the Grouch to their friends.

"Oh, shut up," says Old Mother.

The Grouch and Old Mother are playing Scrabble. The Grouch makes a play.

"Ten points," he says. He is disgusted.

He is angry because Old Mother is winning early in the game and because she has drawn all the s's and blanks. He says it is easy to win if you get all the s's and blanks. "I think you marked the backs," he says. She says a blank tile doesn't have a back.

Now he is angry because she has made the word *qua*. He says *qua* is not English. He says they should both make good, familiar words like the words he has made—*bonnet*, *realm*, and *weave*—but instead she sits in her nasty corner making *aw*, *eh*, *fa*, *ess*, and *ax*. She says these are words, too. He says even if they are, there is something mean and petty about using them.

*   *   *

Now the Grouch is angry because Old Mother keeps freezing all the food he likes. He brings home a nice smoked ham and wants a couple of slices for lunch but it is too late—she has already frozen it.

"It's hard as a rock," he says. "And you don't have to freeze it anyway. It's already smoked."

Then, since everything else he wants to eat is also frozen, he thinks he will at least have some of the chocolate ice cream he bought for her the day before. But it's gone. She has eaten it all.

"Is that what you did last night?" he asks. "You stayed up late eating ice cream?"

He is close to the truth, but not entirely correct.

Old Mother cooks dinner for friends of theirs. After the friends have gone home, she tells the Grouch the meal was a failure: the salad dressing had too much salt in it, the chicken was overdone and tasteless, the cherries hard, etc.

She expects him to contradict her, but instead he listens carefully and adds that the noodles, also, were "somehow wrong."

She says, "I'm not a very good cook."

She expects him to assure her that she is, but instead he says, "You should be. Anybody can be a good cook."

Old Mother sits dejected on a stool in the kitchen.

"I just want to teach you something about the rice pot," says the Grouch, by way of introduction, as he stands at the sink with his back to her.

But she does not like this. She does not wish to be his student.

One night Old Mother cooks him a dish of polenta. He remarks that it has spread on the plate like a cow patty. He tastes it and says that it tastes better than it looks. On another night she makes him a brown rice casserole. The Grouch says this does not look very good either. He covers it in salt and pepper, then eats some of it and says it also tastes better than it looks. Not much better, though.

"Since I met you," says the Grouch, "I have eaten more beans than I ever ate in my life. Potatoes and beans. Every night there is nothing but beans, potatoes, and rice."

Old Mother knows this is not strictly true.

"What did you eat before you knew me?" she asks.

"Nothing," says the Grouch. "I ate nothing."

Old Mother likes all chicken parts, including the liver and heart, and the Grouch likes the breasts only. Old Mother likes the skin on and the Grouch likes it off. Old Mother prefers vegetables and bland food. The Grouch prefers meat and strong spices. Old Mother prefers to eat her food slowly and brings it hot to the table. The Grouch prefers to eat quickly and burns his mouth.

"You don't cook the foods I like," the Grouch tells her sometimes.

"You ought to like the foods I cook," she answers.

"Spoil me. Give me what I want, not what you think

I should have," he tells her.

That's an idea, thinks Old Mother.

Old Mother wants direct answers from the Grouch. But when she asks, "Are you hungry?" he answers, "It's seven o'clock." And when she asks, "Are you tired?" he answers, "It's ten o'clock." And when she insists, and asks again, "But are you tired?" he says, "I've had a long day."

Old Mother likes two blankets at night, on a cold night, and the Grouch is more comfortable with three. Old Mother thinks the Grouch should be comfortable with two. The Grouch, on the other hand, says, "I think you like to be cold."

Old Mother does not mind running out of supplies and often forgets to shop. The Grouch likes to have more than they need of everything, especially toilet paper and coffee.

On a stormy night the Grouch worries about his cat, shut outdoors by Old Mother.

"Worry about me," says Old Mother.

Old Mother will not have the Grouch's cat in the house at night because it wakes her up scratching at the bedroom door or yowling outside it. If they let it into the bedroom, it rakes up the carpet. If she complains about the cat, he takes offense: he feels she is really complaining about him.

Friends say they will come to visit, and then they do not

come. Out of disappointment, the Grouch and Old Mother lose their tempers and quarrel.

On another day, friends say they will come to visit, and this time the Grouch tells Old Mother he will not be home when they come: they are not friends of his.

A phone call comes from a friend of hers he does not like. "It's for you, *angel*," he says, leaving the receiver on the kitchen counter.

Old Mother and the Grouch have quarreled over friends, the West Coast, the telephone, dinner, what time to go to bed, what time to get up, travel plans, her parents, his work, her work, and his cat, among other subjects. They have not quarreled, so far, over special sale items, acquisitions for the house, natural landscapes, wild animals, the town governing board, and the local library.

A woman dressed all in red is jumping up and down in a tantrum. It is Old Mother, who cannot handle frustration.

If Old Mother talks to a friend out of his earshot, the Grouch thinks she must be saying unkind things about him. He is sometimes right, though by the time he appears glowering in the doorway, she has gone on to other topics.

One day in June, the Grouch and Old Mother take all their potted plants out onto the deck for the summer. The next week, the Grouch brings them all back in and sets them on the living room floor. Old Mother does not understand what he is doing and is prepared to object, but they have quarreled and are not speaking to each other, so she can only watch him in silence.

The Grouch is more interested in money than Old Mother and more careful about how he spends it. He reads sale ads and will not buy anything unless it is marked down. "You're not very good with money," he says. She would like to deny it but she can't. She buys a book, secondhand, called *How to Live Within Your Income*.

They spend a good deal of time one day drawing up a list of what each of them will do in their household. For instance, she will make their dinner but he will make his own lunch. By the time they are finished, it is time for lunch and Old Mother is hungry. The Grouch has taken some care over a tuna fish salad for himself. Old Mother says it looks good and asks him if she can share it. Annoyed, he points out that now, contrary to the agreement, he has made *their* lunch.

Old Mother could only have wanted a man of the highest ideals but now she finds she can't live up to them; the Grouch could only have wanted the best sort of woman, but she is not the best sort of woman.

Old Mother thinks her temper may improve if she drinks more water. When her temper remains bad, she begins taking a daily walk and eating more fresh fruit.

Old Mother reads an article which says: If one of you is in a bad mood the other should stay out of her way and be as kind as possible until the bad mood passes.

But when she proposes this to the Grouch, he refuses to consider it. He does not trust her: she will claim to be in a bad mood when she is not, and then require him to be kind to her.

Old Mother decides she will dress up as a witch on Halloween, since she is often described as a witch by the Grouch. She owns a pointed black hat, and now she buys more items to make up her costume. She thinks the Grouch will be amused, but he asks her please to remove the rubber nose from the living room.

The Grouch is exasperated. Old Mother has been criticizing him again. He says to her, "If I changed that, you'd only find something else to criticize. And if I changed that, then something else would be wrong."

The Grouch is exasperated again. Again, Old Mother has been criticizing him. This time he says, "You should have married a man who didn't drink or smoke. And who also had no hands or feet. Or arms or legs."

Old Mother tells the Grouch she feels ill. She thinks she may soon have to go into the bathroom and be sick. They have been quarreling, and so the Grouch says nothing. He goes into the bathroom, however, and washes the toilet bowl, then brings a small red towel and lays it on the foot of the bed where she is resting.

Weeks later, Old Mother tells the Grouch that one of the kindest things he ever did for her was to wash the toilet bowl before she was sick. She thinks he will be touched, but instead, he is insulted.

"Can't you agree with me about anything?" asks the Grouch.

Old Mother has to admit it: she almost always disagrees with him. Even if she agrees with most of what he is saying, there will be some small part of it she disagrees with.

When she does agree with him, she suspects her own motives: she may agree with him only so that at some future time she will be able to remind him that she does sometimes agree with him.

Old Mother has her favorite armchair, and the Grouch has his. Sometimes, when the Grouch is not at home, Old Mother sits in his chair, and then she also picks up what he has been reading and reads it herself.

Old Mother is dissatisfied with the way they spend their evenings together and imagines other activities such as taking walks, writing letters, and seeing friends. She proposes these activities to the Grouch, but the Grouch becomes angry. He does not like her to organize anything in his life. Now the way they spend this particular evening is quarreling over what she has said.

Both the Grouch and Old Mother want to make love,

but he wants to make love before the movie, whereas she wants to make love either during it or after. She agrees to before, but then if before, wants the radio on. He prefers the television and asks her to take her glasses off. She agrees to the television, but prefers to lie with her back to it. Now he can't see it over her shoulder because she is lying on her side. She can't see it because she is facing him and her glasses are off. He asks her to move her shoulder.

Old Mother hears the footsteps of the Grouch in the lower hall as he leaves the living room on his way to bed. She looks around the bedroom to see what will bother him. She removes her feet from his pillow, stands up from his side of the bed, turns off a few lights, takes her slippers out of his way into the room, and shuts a dresser drawer. But she knows she has forgotten something. What he complains about first is the wrinkled sheets, and then the noise of the white mice running in their cage in the next room.

"Maybe I could help with that," says Old Mother sincerely as they are driving in the car, but after what she did the night before she knows he will not want to think of her as a helpful person. The Grouch only snorts.

Old Mother shares a small triumph with the Grouch, hoping he will congratulate her. He remarks that some day she will not bother to feel proud of that sort of thing.

"I slept like a log," he says in the morning. "What about you?"

Well, most of the night was fine, she explains, but toward morning she slept lightly trying to keep still in a position that did not hurt her neck. She was trying to keep still so as not to bother him, she adds. Now he is angry.

"How did you sleep?" she asks him as he comes downstairs late.

"Not very well," he answers. "I was awake around 1:30. You were still up."

"No, I wasn't still up at 1:30," she says.

"12:30, then."

"You were very restless," says the Grouch in the morning. "You kept tossing and turning."

"Don't accuse me," says Old Mother.

"I'm not accusing you, I'm just stating the facts. You were very restless."

"All right: the reason I was restless was that you were snoring."

Now the Grouch is angry. "I don't snore."

Old Mother is lying on the bathroom floor reading, her head on a small stack of towels and a pillow, a bath towel covering her, because she has not been able to sleep and doesn't want to disturb the Grouch. She falls asleep there on the bathroom floor, goes back to bed, wakes again, returns to the bathroom, and continues to read. Finally the Grouch, having woken up because she was gone, comes to the door and offers her some earplugs.

The Grouch wants to listen to Fischer-Dieskau singing, accompanied by Brendel at the piano, but to his annoyance he finds that Fischer-Dieskau accompanied by Brendel is also accompanied by Old Mother humming, and he asks her to stop.

Old Mother makes an unpleasant remark about one of their lamps.

The Grouch is sure Old Mother is insulting him. He tries to figure out what she is saying about him, but can't, and so remains silent.

The Grouch is on his way out with heavy boxes in his arms when Old Mother thinks of something else she wants to say.

"Hurry up, I'm holding these," says the Grouch.

Old Mother does not like to hurry when she has something to say. "Put them down for a minute," she tells him.

The Grouch does not like to be delayed or told what to do. "Just hurry up," he says.

In the middle of an argument, the Grouch often looks at Old Mother in disbelief which is either real or feigned: "What a minute," he says. "Wait just a minute."

Well into an argument, Old Mother often begins to cry in frustration. Though her frustration and her tears are genuine she also hopes the Grouch will be moved to pity. The Grouch is never moved to pity, only further exasperated, saying, "Now you start sniveling."

* * *

The Grouch often arrives home asking such questions as:

"What is this thing? Are you throwing coffee grounds under this bush? Did you mean to leave the car doors unlocked? Do you know why the garage door is open? What is all that water doing on the lawn? Is there a reason all the lights in the house are on? Why was the hose unscrewed?"

Or he comes downstairs and asks:

"Who broke this? Where are all the bath mats? Is your sewing machine working? When did this happen? Did you see the stain on the kitchen ceiling? Why is there a sponge on the piano?"

Old Mother says, "Don't always criticize me."

The Grouch says, "I'm not criticizing you. I just want certain information."

They often disagree about who is to blame: if he is hurt by her, it is possible that she was harsh in what she said; but it is also possible that her intentions were good and he was too sensitive in his reaction.

For instance, the Grouch may be unusually sensitive to the possibility that a woman is ordering him around. But this is hard to decide, because Old Mother is a woman who tends to order people around.

Old Mother is excited because she has a plan to improve her German. She tells the Grouch she is going to listen to Advanced German tapes while she is out driving in the car.

"That sounds depressing," says the Grouch.

The Grouch is cross about his own work when he comes home and therefore cross with her. He snaps at her: "I can't do everything at once."

She is offended and becomes angry. She demands an apology, wanting him to be sincere and affectionate.

He apologizes, but because he is still cross, he is not sincere and affectionate.

She becomes angrier.

Now he complains: "When I'm upset, you get even more upset."

"I'm going to put on some music," says the Grouch.

Old Mother is immediately nervous.

"Put on something easy," she says.

"I know that whatever I put on, you won't like it," he says.

"Just don't put on Messiaen," she says. "I'm too tired for Messiaen."

The Grouch comes into the living room to apologize for what he has said. Then he feels he must explain why he said it, though Old Mother already knows. But as he explains at some length, what he says makes him angry all over again, and he says one or two more things that provoke her, and they begin arguing again.

Now and then Old Mother wonders just why she and the Grouch have such trouble getting along. Perhaps, given her failures of tact, she needed a man with more confidence. Certainly, at the same time, given his extreme sensitivity, he needed a gentler woman.

* * *

They receive many Chinese fortunes. The Grouch finds it correct that her mentality is "alert, practical, and analytical," especially concerning his faults. He finds it correct that "The great fault in women is to desire to be like men," but it has not been true, so far, most of the time anyway, that "Someone you care about seeks reconciliation" or that "She always gets what she wants through her charm and personality."

Certainly the Grouch wanted a strong-willed woman, but not one quite as strong-willed as Old Mother.

The Grouch puts on some music. Old Mother starts crying. It is a Haydn piano sonata. He thought she would like it. But when he put it on and smiled at her, she started crying.

Now they are having an argument about Charpentier and Lully: he says he no longer plays Charpentier motets when she is at home because he knows she does not like them.
She says he still plays Lully.
He says it's the Charpentier motets she doesn't like.
She says it's the whole period she doesn't like.

Now she has put her stamps in his stamp box, thinking to be helpful. But the stamps are of many different denominations and have stuck together in the damp weather. They argue about the stamps, and then go on to argue about the argument. She wants to prove he was unfair to her, since her intentions were good. He wants to prove she was not really thinking of him. But because they cannot agree on the sequence in which certain remarks were made, neither one can convince the other.

The Grouch needs attention, but Old Mother pays attention mainly to herself. She needs attention too, of course, and the Grouch would be happy to pay attention to her if the circumstances were different. He will not pay her much attention if she pays him almost none at all.

Old Mother is in the bathroom for an inordinately long time. When she comes out, the Grouch asks her if she is upset with him. This time, however, she was only picking raspberry seeds out of her teeth.

SAMUEL JOHNSON
IS INDIGNANT:

that Scotland has so few trees.

NEW YEAR'S RESOLUTION

I ask my friend Bob what his New Year's Resolutions are and he says, with a shrug (indicating that this is obvious or not surprising): to drink less, to lose weight... He asks me the same, but I am not ready to answer him yet. I have been studying my Zen again, in a mild way, out of desperation over the holidays, though mild desperation. A medal or a rotten tomato, it's all the same, says the book I have been reading. After a few days of consideration, I think the most truthful answer to my friend Bob would be: My New Year's Resolution is to learn to see myself as nothing. Is this competitive? He wants to lose some weight, I want to learn to see myself as nothing. Of course, to be competitive is not in keeping with any Buddhist philosophy. A true nothing is not competitive. But I don't think I'm being competitive when I say it. I am feeling truly humble, at that moment. Or I think I am—in fact, can anyone be truly humble at the moment they say they want to learn to be nothing? But there is another problem, which I have been wanting to describe to Bob for a few weeks now: at last, halfway through your life, you are smart enough to see that it all amounts to nothing, even success amounts to nothing. But how does a person learn to see herself as nothing when she has already had so much trouble learning to see herself as something in the first place? It's so confusing. You spend the first half of your life learning that you are something after all, now you have to spend the second half learning to see yourself as nothing. You have been a negative nothing, now you want to be a positive nothing. I have begun trying, in these first days of the New Year, but so far it's pretty difficult. I'm pretty close to nothing all morning, but by late afternoon what is in me that is something starts throwing its weight around. This happens many days. By evening, I'm full of something and it's often something nasty and pushy. So what I think at this point is that I'm aiming too high, that maybe nothing is too much, to begin with. Maybe for now I should just try, each day, to be a little less than I usually am.

FIRST GRADE:
HANDWRITING PRACTICE

Were you there when
they crucified my Lord?
Were you there when
they crucified my Lord?
Oh! Sometimes it causes me
to tremble, tremble, tremble.
Were you there when

(turn over)
they crucified my Lord?

INTERESTING

My friend is interesting but he is not in his apartment.

Their conversation appears interesting but they are speaking a language I do not understand.

They are both reputed to be interesting people and so I'm sure their conversation is interesting, but they are speaking a language I understand only a little, so I catch only fragments such as "I see" and "on Sunday" and "unfortunately."

This man has a good understanding of his subject and says many things about it that are probably interesting in themselves, but I am not interested because the subject does not interest me.

Here is a woman I know coming up to me. She is very excited, but she is not an interesting woman. What excites her will not be interesting, it will simply not be interesting.

At a party, a highly nervous man talking fast says many smart things about subjects that do not particularly interest me, such as the restoration of historic houses and in particular the age of wallpaper. Yet, because he is so smart and because he gives me so much information per minute, I do not get tired of listening to him.

Here is a very handsome English traffic engineer. The fact that he is so handsome, and so animated, and has such a fine English accent makes it appear, each time he begins to speak, that he is about to say something interesting, but he is never interesting, and he is saying something, yet again, about traffic patterns.

HAPPIEST MOMENT

If you ask her what is a favorite story she has written, she will hesitate for a long time and then say it may be this story that she read in a book once: an English language teacher in China asked his Chinese student to say what was the happiest moment in his life. The student hesitated for a long time. At last he smiled with embarrassment and said that his wife had once gone to Beijing and eaten duck there, and she often told him about it, and he would have to say the happiest moment of his life was her trip, and the eating of the duck.

JURY DUTY

Q.

A. Jury duty.

Q.

A. The night before, we had been quarreling.

Q.

A. The family.

Q.

A. Four of us. Well, one doesn't live at home anymore. But he was home that night. He was leaving the next morning—the same morning I had to go in to the courtroom.

Q.

A. We were all four of us quarreling. Every which way. I was just now trying to figure it out. There are so many different combinations in which four people can quarrel: one on one, two against one, three against one, two against two, etc. I'm sure we were quarreling in just about every combination.

Q.

A. I don't remember now. Funny. Considering how heated it was.

Q.

A. Well, I put the older boy on the bus, and went on to the courthouse. No, that's not true. He stayed home alone, I trusted him home alone for a couple of hours. He was supposed to catch the bus in front of the house. That worked out all right, he was gone when I came home later. He hadn't taken anything, as far as I could see.

Q.

A. That's a long story.

Q.

A. The younger one was at school and my husband was at work. I had to be at the courthouse at nine. It was a Monday.

Q.

A. I was a little late—I had trouble parking. But of course the parking lot was full because I was already late. Most of the others were there. A couple of people came in after me.

Q.

A. A big old building uptown, very old. It was the same courthouse where Sojourner Truth testified when...

Q.

A. Sojourner Truth.

Q.

A. Sojourner.

Q.

A. She was a former slave who fought for women's rights back in the 1850's. I read that on the historic plaque they have out front. They also said she was illiterate.

Q.

A. Sojourner Truth testified there in that same building, probably in the very same courtroom we were sitting in. Although they didn't say that, come to think of it, and you'd think they would have, since they told us how the room had just been completely restored. In fact they asked us to admire it. That was strange, under the circumstances.

Q.

A. Strange that they would begin talking about the building, the architecture, in the midst of all the instructions they were giving us. As if we were there for a tour, instead of because we had to be there.

Q.

A. It was like a big old library reading room. Or one of those large waiting rooms with high ceilings in an old train station—there's one in New Haven, and there's Grand Central, of course.

Q.

A. Wooden pews, actually. Like a church or an old train station. But comfortable. Surprisingly.

Q.

A. About 175.

Q.

A. They were very quiet. Some of them were reading, some were talking to each other very quietly, just a few. I think they had found someone they knew or they were just being sociable with the person next to them.

Q.

A. No, I didn't talk to any of them, really. There was one older Italian man sitting near me. He couldn't understand anything they said, so I told him what we were supposed to do. He said he used to work in the garment district down in the city. He was a tailor.

Q.

A. Most were just sitting there looking around or staring straight ahead. They were very calm. They were also very alert. I'm sure they felt the same thing I did, that at any moment something might happen, we might be asked to do something, go somewhere. All very expectant, all these people, under that very high ceiling.

Q.

A. Well, first they called the roll—all our names. Most of us were there. Then they told us some of what would be happening. Then we waited.

Q.

A. I don't know—an hour, maybe.

Q.

A. I forget what we were waiting for. Something to do with the judges, or the case. There was a lot of waiting.

Q.

A. Then, after an hour, there was another instruction. I think we were told we could go out for 20 minutes if we wanted a cigarette or to go to the bathroom. I told the Italian man to be sure to come back in 20 minutes.

Q.

A. Someone employed by the court, some officer of the court. I forget if they told us. First it was a man, telling us what the day would be like, roughly, and the week. Then a woman. Still, we didn't really know what to expect. It's funny to think about, but we were all prepared to do what- ever they told us. They could have told us to go to another room and sit there and we would have. Then they could have told us to come back and sit. They could have told half of us to go to another room, and we would have done that. We were very trusting of them.

Q.

A. Very gently. Very calmly, gently. They would say some- thing and then leave, go out some door, come back in, say something else. They would look up from some papers and say something to us almost intimately, as though we weren't a whole crowd. And very respectfully. It was very soothing. As though they were treating us as kindly as possible because they were about to give us some bad news. And we couldn't answer them. We weren't invited to, but we also didn't dare.

Q.

A. No, it wasn't. I thought about that: first I thought of church, then an AA meeting, then something like going to an opera, or a concert. I thought of a large town meeting. But it was different. It was much more peaceful. For one thing, we weren't talking, none of us were talking, really. We weren't supposed to. And also, it was peaceful because we weren't looking for anything, we hadn't come there looking for some kind of spiritual uplift, or rehabilitation. Also, we weren't doing anything, we weren't even waiting for a train, or for an appointment. Actually, we were waiting, but we didn't know what we were waiting for, we didn't know what to expect. So there was this sort of blank wall ahead of us.

Q.

A. A blank wall ahead of us where the rest of the day would normally be, where you could normally see more or less what was coming next.

Q.

A. Yes, but they didn't explain much, and no one dared to ask.

Q.

A. It wasn't emotional. Going to church would be emotion-al. Going to an AA meeting or even a concert would be emotional. This was the most unemotional thing you could imagine. Maybe that's why it was such a relief.

Q.

A. After all that awful quarreling the night before. It was

like some sort of therapy, some sort of treatment. A pre-
scription. As though after such quarreling I was required by
law to report to a place where I had to sit very still with
other people who were sitting very still, and we would all
be treated very kindly and gently until we were completely
well again.

Q.

A. Not the way we do. Not like our family. It scares me. It
scares the pets. God knows what it's doing to my younger
boy.

Q.

A. Yes, we had no choice. We couldn't avoid it. By law, we
had to be there. So there was no possibility of conflict—
should I be here, should I not be here? And they didn't want
us in particular—it wasn't in the least personal, it was random, we had been called randomly. And we weren't here
because we had done anything wrong. We were innocent. In
fact we were more than innocent. We were good. We were
good citizens, good enough to be asked to judge other citizens. The law was saying that we were good. Maybe that's
another reason it felt so deeply soothing. It was not emotional, it was not personal, and yet there was this feeling of
approval. The law thinks you're a good person, or at least
good enough.

Q.

A. Yes, they checked us for weapons down at the side
entrance where we came in. They didn't use the old front
entrance anymore. We went in through some modern, ugly

side doors and down some steps below street level, then we
went up to the second floor in an elevator.

Q.

A. There was a metal detector and a guard who looked into
our bags and purses. He was very kind and gentle, too. He
smiled in a kind way. The sign said something like, "No
weapons beyond this point." So it was as though symboli-
cally, too, we were supposed to leave behind anything we
could fight with. We were not going in there to fight.
Anyone who entered through the metal detector and went
beyond it was not dangerous, almost by definition.

Q.

A. Yes, as though we were in suspension, everything in our
lives suspended, waiting. We were waiting.

Q.

A. Yes, I thought of the word patient. But it wasn't that.
Patience is something you need in a strained situation, a situation in which you have to put up with something uncomfortable or difficult. This wasn't difficult. That's what I'm
trying to say: we had to be there, and so it relieved us of all
personal responsibility. I don't think there is anything else
quite like it. Then you have to add onto that the spacious-
ness of the room. Imagine if it had been a small, crowded
room with a low ceiling. Or if people had been noisy, talk-
ative. Or if the people in charge had been confused, or rude.

Q.

A. Finally. The woman had a drum with all our names in it.

She turned the drum and then picked names out of the drum one at a time to go up and sit in the jury box and be interviewed. This was going to be the interesting part—that's what I was thinking.

Q.

A. No, we all had to stay there. All the rest of us had to stay there in case the ones being questioned were disqualified or excused. Since it was random, any one of us might be called up to replace them, so we all had to stay.

Q.

A. Again, very gently, very respectfully. And calling them by their first names, gently, like a doctor or a nurse.

Q.

A. There was an unexpected sort of excitement to it. Something ceremonious. The suspense before she called out the name—everyone thinking it might be their name next, of course. Then when the names were called, they had to go up there in front of all these people, and then they had to answer these personal questions with everyone listening and watching them. There were so many of us. We had no idea who all these people were. Then the lives of some of us were gradually revealed, all the rest of us sitting there and listening. We would hear about these people, we would hear their stories. Now we knew the names of some of them. It was like some Indian ritual, some Navajo ceremony.

Q.

A. Oh, some questions you'd expect, some general questions, like, Are you employed? What do you do for a living? Do you have a family? Then more specific questions. Do you drive? Have you ever been in an accident? Do you have any relatives on the police force? Do you have any relatives in the insurance business? Are you familiar with the Palisades Parkway?

Q.

A. The part just north of Exit 11.

Q.

A. It took a long time. I couldn't hear very well.

Q.

A. Very calmly. They called them by their first names. And there were all these pauses. Question. Pause. One lawyer would consult another lawyer while everyone waited, so quiet, so obedient. These quiet voices, and then long silences, and this expectant atmosphere.

Q.

A. Well, so first they were special, the Chosen. Up in front of everyone. I heard enough of their answers to decide I liked them, or I didn't like them. One woman was a real estate dealer, divorced, a cold, tense sort of woman. Grim. I didn't like her. Then there was a tall strong man, an artist, a family man, obviously a nice guy. I liked him right away. There was a college student who was afraid he'd miss too many days of classes, but then they pointed out to him that this was going to be a short trial and he might miss even more if he didn't go ahead and sit on this jury. So he decided to stay on the jury. And once he was on the jury you had to see him as rather special because he was so young—he was like the child on the jury, the child prodigy, young but wise enough to stand in judgment, who would be taken care of by the older people. And then after a while you even began to dislike him and resent him for being so young, for presuming, for saying in front of everyone that he might not do this thing that he had been asked to do, then for being the child prodigy, so young and bright and being taken care of by the others.

So these ones, who stayed on the jury, they were the Chosen. And the ones who were excused, after all that questioning, when they were excused, when they had to walk back to their seats in front of everybody, they became the Unchosen, they lost all that special prestige, they were ordinary again, they were not special anymore. Or rather, the ones who were rejected for obvious or technical reasons were simply ordinary. But the ones who were rejected for mysterious reasons, for reasons that probably said something not so good about their lives and who they were, they were not just ordinary anymore, now, they had somehow been declared unfit. The others were still sitting up there.

Q.

A. No, not many. Three or four, maybe. One, I think, because he was unemployed and hadn't driven for eleven years—no, longer than that, not since 1979. He used a bicycle to get around. It also came out that he had been in an accident in 1979, or caused one. He had been sued, but he had won. You only get part of the story.

Q.

A. He was dressed more formally than most of the others, in a dark suit and a tie. But his hair was long, in a ponytail, and he was wearing tinted glasses. They asked him about his glasses.

Q.

A. I wasn't surprised that they excused him. He was unemployed. And it also turned out that he wasn't married and had no children. But they don't have to say why they're excusing them. I wondered what he was feeling when he went back to his seat, and after that, for the rest of the day. He was so carefully dressed I thought he might have felt proud that he had been called for jury duty in the first place. Then he might have been embarrassed or humiliated that they didn't want him after all.

Q.

A. Yes, another one was excused because he had a nephew on the police force.

Q.

A. Well, they were all selected by lunchtime, and we were allowed to leave for an hour. They pinned special badges on the ones who had been selected for the jury and instructed them not to talk to anyone, and told us not to talk to them.

Q.

A. Yes. I happened to go to the same café as one of the jurors, and I smiled at her, and she smiled back at me, she knew why I was smiling, she seemed nice, but I didn't dare even say hi.

Q.

A. Yes, we did see some. I think they were brought in from next door. I think the jail was next door and maybe there was an underground passage. Anyway, as far as I can remember, when I first went in, in the morning, I was waiting for the elevator when a line of them came out of another door in the hallway there, in the basement, and went up the stairs next to the elevator. There was one policeman in front of them and one policeman behind them. Then, when we all went out at lunchtime, going back down in the elevator and back out those side doors, they were also being taken back downstairs again and back through that door in the basement hallway. Then, when we came back in from lunch, they were being taken up again. I didn't see them when we left in the afternoon. I guess they were in a courtroom.

Q.

A. There were four or five of them, all men, in orange suits. They were wearing handcuffs and each one was carrying a manila folder, holding it in front of him. They weren't talking, and they looked pretty subdued. They were walking in a line, single file. They all had to keep their arms and hands, and those manila folders, in the same position because of the handcuffs. So they were a little like a show on stage, coordinated.

Q.

A. Yes, it made me feel even more that I was good, or that I was not bad. That it was all very simple, some people were good and some people were not so good. There were people who were proceeding correctly with their lives, and this could be proved by asking them a few questions. And there were people who were not proceeding correctly with their lives.

Q.

A. Though you sensed a bond with the others, when you were all standing around outside during a break. The feeling that you were all in this together, thrown together by chance.

Q.

A. Yes, at lunchtime, when we all went out at once, it reminded me of something and I wasn't sure what. Then I realized it was ladybugs. You can order a package of ladybugs and you get a few hundred in the package. You keep them in the refrigerator until the warm weather comes, and then you release them to feed in your yard. Some of them stay nearby and feed, and some fly away. That's how it was. We were released all at the same time into the neighborhood, nearly two hundred of us, most of us not knowing the neighborhood, and we went out and looked for a place to eat. Most of us stayed and ate near the courthouse.

Q.

A. It was two o'clock when we finally went home. They had us waiting there after lunch in case there was going to be a selection for another trial, but there wasn't another selection, so they let us go. They told us to call that night after six, and to call each night after that for the rest of the week, to see if we had to come in the next day. I called every night for the rest of the week, but I didn't have to go in again. In a way, that felt like therapy too, or some kind of discipline. As though I had to be prepared to do the job again, and if I was prepared, and did the right thing, I might be excused from doing the job. So I did the right thing, each night, and each night I was excused and allowed to stay home the next day.

Q.

A. No, not really. I would have liked to be on a jury. I would have been very interested. But at the same time I had a lot of work I was supposed to be doing at home.

Q.

A. Yes, that was all. I didn't have to do anything more. And I won't be eligible again for two years.

Q.

A. Yes!

A DOUBLE NEGATIVE

At a certain point in her life, she realizes it is not so much
that she wants to have a child as that she does not want not
to have a child, or not to have had a child.

THE OLD DICTIONARY

I have an old dictionary, about one hundred and twenty years old, that I need to use for a particular piece of work I'm doing this year. Its pages are brownish in the margins and brittle, and very large. I risk tearing them when I turn them. When I open the dictionary I also risk tearing the spine, which is already split more than halfway up. I have to decide, each time I think of consulting it, whether it is worth damaging the book further in order to look up a particular word. Since I need to use it for this work, I know I will damage it, if not today, then tomorrow, and that by the time I am done with this work it will be in poorer condition than it was when I started, if not completely ruined. When I took it off the shelf today, though, I realized that I treat it with a good deal more care than I treat my young son. Each time I handle it, I take the greatest care not to harm it: my primary concern is not to harm it. What struck me today was that even though my son should be more important to me than my old dictionary, I can't say that each time I deal with my son, my primary concern is not to harm him. My primary concern is almost always something else, for instance to find out what his homework is, or to get supper on the table, or to finish a phone conversation. If he gets harmed in the process, that doesn't seem to matter to me as much as getting the thing done, whatever it is. Why don't I treat my son at least as well as the old dictionary? Maybe it is because the dictionary is so obviously fragile. When a corner of a page snaps off, it is unmistakable. My son does not look fragile, bending over a game or manhandling the dog. Certainly his body is strong and flexible, and is not easily harmed by me. I have bruised his body and then it has healed. Sometimes it is obvious to me when I have hurt his feelings, but it is harder to see how badly they have been hurt, and they seem to mend. It is hard to see if they mend completely or are forever slightly damaged. When the dictionary is hurt, it can't be mended. Maybe I treat the dictionary better because it makes no demands on me, and doesn't fight back. Maybe I am kinder to things that don't seem to react to me. But in fact my house plants do not seem to react much and yet I don't treat them very well. The plants make one or two demands. Their demand for light has already been satisfied by where I put them. Their second demand is for water. I water them but not regularly. Some of them don't grow very well because of that and some of them die. Most of them are strange-looking rather than nice-looking. Some of them were nice-looking when I bought them but are strange-looking now because I haven't taken very good care of them. Most of them are in pots that are the same ugly plastic pots they came in. I don't actually like them very much. Is there any other reason to like a houseplant, if it is not nice-looking? Am I kinder to something that is nice-looking? But I could treat a plant well even if I didn't like its looks. I should be able to treat my son well when he is not looking good and even when he is not acting very nice. I treat the dog better than the plants, even though he is more active and more demanding. It is simple to give him food and water. I take him for walks, though not often enough. I have also sometimes slapped his nose, though the vet told me never to hit him anywhere near the head, or maybe he said anywhere at all. I am only sure I am not neglecting the dog when he is asleep. Maybe I am kinder to things that are not alive. Or rather if they are not alive there is no question of kindness. It does not hurt them if I don't pay attention to them, and that is a great relief. It is such a relief it is even a pleasure. The only change they show is that they gather dust. The dust won't really hurt them. I can even get someone else to dust them. My son gets dirty, and I can't clean him, and I can't pay someone to clean him. It is hard to keep him clean, and even complicated trying to feed him. He doesn't sleep enough, partly because I try so hard to get him to sleep. The plants need two things, or maybe three. The dog needs five or six things. It is very clear how many things I am giving him and how many I am not, therefore how well I'm taking care of him. My son needs many other things besides what he needs for his physical care, and these things multiply or change constantly. They can change right in the middle of a sentence. Though I often know, I do not always know just what he needs. Even when I know, I am not always able to give it to him. Many times each day I do not give him what he needs. Some of what I do for the old dictionary, though not all, I could do for my son. For instance, I handle it slowly, deliberately, and gently. I consider its age. I treat it with respect. I stop and think before I use it. I know its limitations. I do not encourage it to go farther than it can go (for instance to lie open flat on the table). I leave it alone a good deal of the time.

HONORING THE SUBJUNCTIVE

It invariably precedes, even if it do not altogether supercede, the determination of what is absolutely desirable and just.

HOW DIFFICULT

For years my mother said I was selfish, careless, irresponsible, etc. She was often annoyed. If I argued, she held her hands over her ears. She did what she could to change me but for years I did not change, or if I changed, I could not be sure I had, because a moment never came when my mother said, "You are no longer selfish, careless, irresponsible, etc." Now I'm the one who says to myself, "Why can't you think of others first, why don't you pay attention to what you're doing, why don't you remember what has to be done?" I am annoyed. I sympathize with my mother. How difficult I am! But I can't say this to her, because at the same time that I want to say it, I am also here on the phone coming between us, listening and prepared to defend myself.

LOSING MEMORY

You ask me about Edith Wharton.
Well, the name is very familiar.

LETTER TO A
FUNERAL PARLOR

Dear Sir,

I am writing to you to object to the word *cremains*, which was used by your representative when he met with my mother and me two days after my father's death.

We had no objection to your representative, personally, who was respectful and friendly and dealt with us in a sensitive way. He did not try to sell us an expensive urn, for instance.

What startled and disturbed us was the word *cremains*. You in the business must have invented this word and you are used to it. We the public do not hear it very often. We don't lose a close friend or a family member very many times in our life, and years pass in between, if we are lucky. Even less often do we have to discuss what is to be done with a family member or close friend after their death.

We noticed that before the death of my father you and your representative used the words *loved one* to refer to him. That was comfortable for us, even if the ways in which we loved him were complicated.

Then we were sitting there in our chairs in the living room trying not to weep in front of your representative, who was opposite us on the sofa, and we were very tired first from sitting up with my father, and then from worrying about whether he was comfortable as he was dying, and then from worrying about where he might be now that he was dead, and your representative referred to him as "the cremains."

At first we did not even know what he meant. Then, when we realized, we were frankly upset. *Cremains* sounds like something invented as a milk substitute in coffee, like Cremora, or Coffee-mate. Or it sounds like some kind of a chipped beef dish.

As one who works with words for a living, I must say that any invented word, like *Porta-potty* or *Pooper-scooper*, has a cheerful or even jovial ring to it that I don't think you really intended when you invented the word cremains. In fact, my father himself, who was a professor of English and is now being called *the cremains*, would have pointed out to you the alliteration in *Porta Potti* and the rhyme in *pooper-scooper*. Then he would have told you that *cremains* falls into the same category as *brunch* and is known as a portmanteau word.

There is nothing wrong with inventing words, especially in a business. But a grieving family is not prepared for this one. We are not even used to our loved one being gone. You could very well continue to employ the term *ashes*. We are used to it from the Bible, and are even comforted by it. We would not misunderstand. We would know that these ashes are not like the ashes in a fireplace.

Yours sincerely.

THYROID DIARY

Tonight we are going to a party to celebrate my dentist's wife's graduation from college. All these years, while the dentist has been working on my teeth, his wife has been earning credits at the college, just a few at a time. Every semester, along with her other courses, she has been studying painting with my husband, who teaches painting and drawing at the college. She has been studying with him in a tutorial situation. She is an enthusiastic flower gardener and paints mostly flowers. She has written texts about her flower gardens, to go with her paintings. My husband told me that a flower painting of hers that was hanging in the Art Building at commencement time was stolen—by a student, he thought, or a student's parents.

I didn't know she was actually earning a degree until we received the invitation to this party to be given by her friend, who is a faculty secretary at the college. A few days after the invitation arrived, we received another one from the same woman, but for a different date. I was sure there had been a mistake. But in fact she is simply giving two parties, and we are invited to both.

Now I have to wonder why my serious and extensive dental work ended—which it did—just a couple of months before the dentist's wife's graduation. When the dentist said I didn't need any further work, I thought I still had at least two more crowns to go. I can't remember a time when I haven't had more work to be done on my teeth.

I have always been puzzled, anyway, by the economics of the thing, because I would pay the dentist, and he would presumably give his wife the money for her courses at the college, she would pay the college, the college would pay my husband a separate fee for her tutorials, and then my husband would give me money for the dentist, I would pay the dentist, the dentist would give money to his wife, and so it would continue. I thought that if no one paid anyone, it would work out just the same, but that didn't seem quite right, either.

This spring the dentist, who is a gardener like his wife, but grows vegetables and grapes, and has a small apple orchard, made the transactions a little more complicated by proposing to my husband that they share certain shipments of bedding plants which could be bought more economically in large quantities. He said they might share two varieties of tomatoes as well as some onions and peppers. My husband thought it over and then agreed. In general he is wary of the obligations of any sort of partnership, but he is also interested in saving money, and in this case he appreciated the gesture of goodwill and trust.

The party we are going to tonight will be at the home of the faculty secretary in a small town on the other side of the river. But as soon as I say that, I realize I have made a mistake. This is not the party in honor of the dentist's wife, but the other one. This one is for the faculty secretary's nephew, who is going off on a long sea voyage. After many years of living sometimes on land and sometimes on the water, he has sold his house and will be living on his sailboat, though he still has a girlfriend here on land. I should have remembered this, because my husband and I were just discussing at lunch what to give him as a going-away present. We were considering three choices: a copy of Richard Henry Dana's *Two Years Before the Mast*, or a book that my husband saw about tying knots, or a bottle of wine. My husband also suggested a bottle of good brandy, but I thought that would only encourage our friend to drink alone on his boat.

If I'm confused about all this, it may be because of my underactive thyroid. Slow thinking is one symptom of an underactive thyroid, but I can't tell if I'm thinking more slowly than I used to. Since my brain is the only thing I have for observing how I am thinking, I can't be truly objective. If it is slow, it will not necessarily know that it's slow, since it will be moving at a rate that seems appropriate to it.

And then, there have always been days when my mind does not make connections very fast. There are always days when my mind is cloudy, or I forget things, or I feel as if I am in a different town or a different house—that something around me or about me is not normal.

When the doctor was explaining my condition to me, I took notes. I had to stop her once or twice and ask her to repeat something so that I could write it down. I told her it helped me to remember. She said I would not have to take notes if my thyroid were more active. That made me a little angry, but I did not try to defend myself. I did not answer her that for one thing, the self-help medical books always tell you to take notes during a meeting with a doctor, and for another I have a habit of taking notes anyway, especially when I am on the telephone, and even during conversations when it is not at all necessary, when the information I am hearing is something that does not have to be remembered. I take notes on things I have just said to someone else. I write down words I have just used myself, like *nice guy* or *responsible*. I write down names of people in my family, and my own telephone number.

I did notice, one evening when I was playing a board game with my family, that over and over again I could not remember whose turn it was or see where my piece was on the board. This could have been due to my underactive thyroid.

I thought I wasn't worried about my thyroid, because I believed I could correct whatever problem there was with a strategy involving diet. But maybe I am worried after all, because for the past week, ever since my doctor called me, I haven't been sleeping well. My trouble sleeping, though, may be due to the underactive thyroid.

My doctor is not actually a doctor, as my husband is quick to say: she's only a physician's assistant. He says this as though she may not know what she's talking about. He says this in my defense, as though to protect me from her or from my condition. But I think she's careful and competent, and I believe her. Now I'm eating only vegetables for dinner, preparing to begin my dietary strategy. I truly believe the body can cure itself of whatever is wrong with it, given the right diet and other treatments. I am only waiting for some more tests, which I will have this week, before I make a plan for my care. I'm sure that whatever diet I choose, I should not drink any alcohol, but I have already planned to make an exception for the party tonight.

My physician's assistant told me the thyroid gland controls every part of the body—not only the brain but also the heart, the digestion, the metabolism, the circulation, and other things I may be forgetting. In the case of a significantly underactive thyroid, everything slows down. I have a slow heartbeat, slow digestion, possibly slow thinking, a low temperature, cold hands and feet. Sometimes my heart rate goes down to fifty or below. I never knew what a thyroid gland did. Now I find out it is so important that if it were allowed to continue functioning poorly like this, I would eventually die—die early, I mean. I have never associated myself with such an unexpected part of the body as the thyroid, so it feels as though my body is suddenly strange to me, or I am strange to myself.

Now I have learned more about what is wrong with me, and I do not think the body can always cure itself of whatever is wrong with it. Or rather, I still believe this as a general principle, but I don't think my body can cure itself in this case, because no one seems to know enough about this particular disease, which is an auto-immune disease. It is called Hashimoto's disease, though my husband keeps calling it Kurasawa's, or Nagasaki's.

By now I have also been to the first party, given for our sailor friend, as well as the second party, given for our dentist's wife. The parties were very different even though they were at the same house. In the perennial beds, different flowers were in bloom. The first party was informal, as was appropriate for a going-away party for a sailor. Neighbors wearing casual clothes came out onto the lawn from short-cuts through the woods. At the second, there were trays of catered hors d'oeuvres and a uniformed serving woman. At that party I learned that not one, but two, of the dentist's wife's paintings had been stolen at commencement time. I learned that the paintings were much smaller than I had thought. One from the same series was hanging on the wall in the faculty secretary's house. It was small enough to put in your pocket or your purse. The dentist was sitting in a wicker chair on the screened porch. I did not find it strange to see him there instead of in his office, but I also couldn't smile at him socially in quite the same way I would at any-one else, since he knows my teeth so well, particularly my upper left incisor.

A corkscrew willow grows by a tiny stream in the front yard of the faculty secretary's house. At the first party, she cut a shoot of the corkscrew willow for me to take home and plant. I forgot to take it. From the second, I took several more shoots, but at home I put them in a bucket of water in the garage and forgot them for a few days. I then offered them to a friend, but forgot to give them to her, and the water in the bucket evaporated and they withered.

I have also been up to see a specialist in Albany several times, more often than was necessary, my husband believes. My husband thinks the specialist could simply read the numbers and look at the results of the blood tests, and that like other doctors he schedules extra office visits to make more money. But a friend of mine said, "With gland problems, they like to look at you." I do not remember which friend it was.

And yet this specialist seemed to avoid looking at me. At least he avoided it when he first walked into the room— he looked down at my file instead. He did eventually look at me, with his head cocked a little to one side and a slight smile on his face that seemed to express a private amusement that was not completely unfriendly. But he looked at me only when he was ready to deliver his opinion, which he had already formed by reading the numbers in my file.

Meanwhile, my husband has been having trouble with his tomato plants. The dentist gave him four or five healthy, well-grown plants, neatly potted in peat pots, and they are doing well. In return, my husband is supposed to give him four or five of another variety. But most of these arrived in the mail half dead. Some died, two are doing fairly well, and the rest are not dead, but are not growing, either, at least not visibly. My husband does not want to give away the only two that are thriving. He also does not want to give the dentist spindly and sickly plants. He is waiting, time is passing, but the plants that were not growing well are not growing any better.

I have been trying to see if I am thinking more slowly than before. In my translation work, for instance, I see that I sometimes try to find an equivalent in English before I really understand the French. Then I realize that I don't understand the French, even after trying several times, and I cast my eye rather listlessly here and there within the paragraph hoping the meaning of it will fall into place by itself, which it sometimes does. But today it does not, and then my mind wanders. I go back to work on it, look in the dictionary again, reading every word of a very long entry, but there's nothing in the dictionary that helps me. I want to put something down, anything at all, just to mark the place so that I can go on translating and come back to the problem later. I need to put down something noticeably wrong, so that later I will see that the spot needs work, but everything I think of is so poor that it is embarrassing. I don't know why I should be embarrassed, if there is no one to see it, but I am embarrassed and will not go on until I put down something decent, though wrong. At least, this morning, as I was studying the dictionary carefully in order to see if I really wanted to use the word, I learned more about *embarrassment* and its earlier, concrete meaning of *encumbrance* or *obstruction*.

But then, even though I had been awake since six o'clock and had been working for an hour already, someone who didn't know me, in fact someone from the doctor's office, said to me on the phone, "Sounds like you're not up yet. Can you call me back when you are?" I was not insulted, but I was a little worried. I apparently sounded very slow on the phone, even if I did not think I was very slow. Now, if I do this whole translation, which is an important job, with my mind not working very clearly, but not knowing that my mind isn't working very clearly, then the translation may not be very good—though I may not know that. And if it isn't very good—that would really be unfortunate, since some of my future income may depend on it.

Actually, what the receptionist or nurse took to be slowness may be something else, an attitude I now have that is more casual toward health-care professionals. I used to be very respectful of them and slightly intimidated. Now I have noticed that I want to make fun of the men and joke with the women, or I should say, joke with both men and women, but rather more aggressively with the men.

I first noticed this a few years ago with my oral surgeon. I liked him and respected him, but I noticed after a while that I would not deal in a straightforward, courteous way with him, but had to make some kind of a joke. That shocked me, because all my life I have been so respectful of health-care professionals, or have at least behaved with respect, whatever I thought of them privately. The jokes just popped out as though someone else had taken over for a moment. Once, for instance, I saw a skull in his office and made what was no doubt the obvious joke—that it must be a former patient. He was startled, but did not seem to mind. Another time, when he had just hurt me badly by giving me a long injection in my gum, I bit down hard on his index finger. That was not a joke, and I did not do it on purpose. His two female assistants were amazed but also delighted. Although he frowned in pain and shook his finger in the air, the doctor took it very well and said it happened from time to time, that it was actually a reflex. I slightly antagonized my present doctor, or physician's assistant, by saying that I did not like taking medicine because I did not like being dependent on any drug. What if I were lost in a jungle without my thyroid medicine? I asked her, and it is true that I always believe that some day I may be lost in a jungle, even though we do not call them jungles anymore, and we are losing them anyway, so that the word *jungle* is becoming just an idea. She said I would get along well enough without it until I could find my way out of the jungle.

There was a small emergency situation quite recently, though, in which I was not tempted to make fun of the doctor. He was a young doctor, I admired his decisiveness and his technical skill, and I was also quiet because of my pain. I had bruised my finger badly, and what he had to do was to release some of the pressure under the nail. He did this in what he said was the best way, but also the old-fashioned way, using nothing but a candle and a large paper clip.

The receptionist or nurse this morning thought I wasn't "up" yet because I didn't know the exact dose or the full name of my thyroid medicine. But I was careless about that information because of my skeptical attitude toward the health-care profession and because I do not try to conceal that attitude. I did not mean to be disrespectful to her in particular. But after she said this, I noticed two other possible signs of poor functioning: a real estate dealer I called on the phone later in the morning thought at first that I was another real estate dealer. I asked her why she thought this. She had trouble answering, but I guessed that it might have been my lack of enthusiasm, or a coldness in my tone of voice. Then, still later, when I was talking to my husband on the telephone, I was so confusing, contradictory, and long-winded that he compared me to a legal brief he was reading. This document is fifty pages long and concerns a possible class action against an insurance company for misrepresentation.

After wondering for some weeks what to do about the

tomato plants, my husband told me he was going to explain to the dentist that none of the plants was good enough to give him, though that is not strictly true. Then, just hours later, he told me that he had changed his mind. He was going to patch the soaker hose and give the plants a little more time.

But on the other hand, it occurs to me that maybe my brain is working well enough but simply more slowly than usual. Maybe the quality of my work will be good but I will take longer than usual to make it good. Or maybe the dose of thyroid supplement I'm taking, which has been increased once without much effect, will be increased to the proper level soon enough so that by the time I reach the final draft of this translation I will be thinking sharply and quickly again. Then I wonder if I will think even better than before this whole condition began, because my brain will have been trying so hard in the meantime, without adequate support from my thyroid, that maybe it will have developed new cells. But I don't know enough about the brain's anatomy to know if that is possible.

Or maybe some of the time I go ahead quickly enough but without producing very high quality work, while some of the time I go ahead slowly and produce better quality work, so that it is a choice: either go slowly and do good work, or go quickly and do poor work. But then, those have always been the two options in translation, I see, so I should say that now the choice is: go even more slowly than before and do adequately good work, or go more quickly and do really poor work.

But with any luck, the dosage will gradually be raised

high enough so that in a couple of months I will be able to do work that is both quick and adequately good or quite good. The dosage can't be raised too abruptly or my heart will suffer.

I had thought at first, If my brain is working this well with inadequate amounts of thyroid hormone, how well my brain will work with the proper amounts of thyroid hormone! But then I began to distrust the thought, because what seemed like good working of the brain seemed good to that very same brain that was lacking the proper dose of hormone, and that brain could be quite mistaken.

Another question I had recently was this: is the rather pessimistic turn that my thoughts have taken these days due to the state of the world, which is bad and which gets worse more quickly than one can hope to save it, so that I become quite scared? Or is it due simply to the low level of my thyroid hormone, which would mean that maybe the world is not really in such a frightening state and seems that way only to me? So that I could say to myself: Remember your low thyroid hormone level and have faith that the world will be all right?

What an insult to the mind, I think then, that the chemicals of the body and nothing else are causing my thoughts, which I take so seriously, to move in a certain direction. What an insult to the amazing brain that such a simple thing as a level of chemicals should point it in a certain direction. Then I think, No, it's not an insult, I can think of it not as an insult, but as part of another fascinating system. I can say, I would prefer to see it as part of a single, interesting system. Then I think, And, after all, it is this amazing brain that, in thinking this, is being so magnanimous to the dumb body. Though of course maybe it is the chemicals of the dumb body that are permitting the amazing brain to be magnanimous.

Now I have been to the dentist again for a cleaning and checkup, and he has found a large cracked filling in a tooth that he said should really have a crown or a cap. He said he had predicted this years ago. But when I objected to more major work, and asked for a postponement, he consented to treat it with a bonded filling that might or might not last for a long time. I was a little surprised that he agreed to this. I wondered if he was losing his enthusiasm, or losing the conviction—which all my dentists seem to have had—that all work on my teeth should be as extreme and as complete as possible. I also noticed that he was curiously silent about tomatoes, saying nothing, either, about the other vegetables in his garden, or about his harvests. We talked instead about crowded holiday spots and the westward expansion of the United States during the nineteenth century. His grandfather had actually lived in the days of the westward expansion and used to talk to him about it. He said it was surprising how recent that time was.

Our talk extended out into the reception area while I paid my bill and took a pencil from the box of gift pencils. Considering the rapid population growth, he said, he did not want to come back after he died. I agreed that I would not want to come back either, at least not as a person, adding the qualification, which I believe, that if we have to come back we may be safer coming back as cockroaches. The receptionist and dental hygienist, who were listening, looked surprised at this.

Now that the fall semester has begun, the woman who gave both parties is back at work at the college. Nearly every day, I read notices that she sends out to all the faculty. She has a very sharp and funny mind, a good education, and an interesting background, but her notices are deliberately neutral in tone and strictly practical. Some are about empty cardboard boxes free for the taking, some about stray cats on the campus, and a great many about misuse of the Xerox machines. Only now and then can I detect from something she says about a page of sonnets left in her office, or from her rhetorically balanced sentences, or from her use of the word *criterion*, how sharp she is.

Since the dentist's wife now has her degree, she is no longer studying with my husband, but I do not remember what she is doing, though I was told, probably by my husband.

We have been eating the tomatoes from our garden, though the harvest is not as good as it has been in other years. A woodchuck has dug a hole down under the fence and up among the tomato plants and has been eating the tomatoes as they ripen. My husband puts heavy stones in the hole, but during the night the woodchuck moves them.

I thought this was the end of it, that I would hear no more about the dentist and the results of the season's planting. I thought there was a slight embarrassment all around. But last week my husband came home from his three-month cleaning with a bag of onions and told me that the issue had been tacitly resolved, that he and the dentist had talked about the long dry spells coming at the wrong times and how the summer had been a poor one for tomatoes. Even the dentist's plants had not done well. And yesterday, during the insertion of my bonded filling, the dentist told me how he makes grape jelly. I am relieved that there are apparently no hard feelings. The dentist's onions are pretty, small and fresh. I will want to think of some way of preparing them so that they will be particularly noticeable as we eat them.

My heart seems to be beating a little faster now. If it is true that I have been thinking more slowly, I have still been able to learn new things and remember them, in the past few months. I forget what we actually gave to our sailor friend, and there are other things I know I have forgotten, and still others that I must have forgotten, but I have learned the history of the word *embarrassment* and many other word histories, I have been introduced to the corkscrew willow, I have learned the term *bonded filling*, and many other new definitions from the dictionaries, for instance that the verb *flense* means *to cut up a whale*, and that the adjective *next* is the superlative of *nigh*. I have learned two new terms for familiar things: in music, the *Alberti bass*, and in grammar, the *Oxford comma*. I have had new thoughts about the westward expansion of the United States. I have heard the expression *dead soldiers* twice in two days and learned that it means empty bottles. Maybe it also means anything that is no more use to anyone, since I first heard it from a woman at a plant nursery who was looking through a bin of gourds and tossing out the rotten ones. I learned from the dentist that if I make grape jelly I should heat the sugar in the oven before adding it to the grape juice. I have learned more about the Kennedy family and particularly Edward Kennedy from a magazine in the dentist's office. I had no trouble, after a few minutes, recognizing Dvořák's "New World Symphony" on the radio while I was having my bonded filling put in. After reading the introduction again, having read it years ago and forgotten what I learned from it, I have learned yet again how Richard Henry Dana's *Two Years Before the Mast* came to be written, that when Dana was a student at Harvard he fell ill and could not continue his studies, went to sea to recover his health, and subsequently wrote about his experiences, so that it is the book of a young man, whereas I had thought of it as the book of an older man just because it has been a classic for so many decades. What I don't know yet is why I see it so often in secondhand bookstores and at library sales.

INFORMATION FROM THE NORTH
CONCERNING THE ICE:

Each seal uses many blowholes and each blowhole is used by many seals.

MURDER IN BOHEMIA

In the city of Frydlant in Bohemia where all the people are anyway pale as ghosts and dressed in dark winter clothes, an old woman was unable any longer to bear the inevitable falling of her life into destitution and disgrace, and went mad and murdered out of pity her husband, her two sons, and her daughter, out of anger her neighbors on one side and her neighbors across the street, who had scorned her family, out of revenge the grocer from whom she had had to beg for credit, and the pawnbroker, and two moneylenders, then a streetcar conductor whom she did not know, and finally— rushing with her long knife into the Town Hall—the young mayor and one of his councilmen as they sat puzzling over an amendment.

HAPPY MEMORIES

I imagine that when I am old, I will be alone, and in pain, and my eyes will be too weak to read. I am afraid of those long days. I like my days to be happy. I try to think what would be a happy way to spend those difficult days. It may be that the radio will be enough to fill those days. An old person has her radio, I have heard it said. And I have heard it said that in addition to her radio, she has her happy memories. When her pain is not too bad, she can go over her happy memories and be comforted. But you must have happy memories. What bothers me is that I'm not sure how many happy memories I will have. I am not even sure just what makes a happy memory, the kind that will both comfort me and give me pleasure when I can't do anything else. Just because I enjoy something now does not mean that it will make a happy memory. In fact, I know that many of the things I enjoy now will not make good happy memories later. I am happy doing the work I do, alone at a desk. That work is a great part of every day. But when I am old and alone all the time, will it be enough to think about the work

I used to do? Another thing I enjoy is eating candy by myself while I read a book in the evening, but I don't think that will make a good happy memory either. I like to play the piano, I like to look at the plants that come up in the yard beginning in March, I enjoy walking with my dog, and looking down into his face at his good eye and his bad eye, I like to see the sky in the late afternoon, especially in November, I like petting my cats, hearing their cries, and holding them. But I suspect that the memory of my pets will not be enough, either, even if I love them. There are things that make me laugh, but often they are grim things, and they will not make a good happy memory either, unless I share them with someone else. Then it is not the amusement but the sharing of it that makes the happy memory. It seems as though a happy memory has to involve other people. I think of all the different people. I think of the good encounters with people. Most of the people I talk to on the telephone are friendly, even when I have called a wrong number. I have a happy memory of stopping my car by the side of the road to talk to a woman about her garden. I talk to the people who work in the post office and the drugstore, and I used to talk to the people at the bank before they put an automated teller machine in the lobby. When a man came to fix the dehumidifier in the basement, we talked about the history of this town. I enjoy my conversations with the librarian down the street. I enjoy the friendly messages I receive from bookstores selling secondhand books. But I don't think any of these encounters will make a memory that will comfort me when I am old. Maybe a happy memory can't involve people who were only strangers or casual friends. You can't be left alone, in your old age and pain, with memories that include only people who have forgotten you. The people in your happy memories have to be the same people who want to have you in their own happy memories. A lively dinner party does not make a good happy memory if no one there cared very much for any of the others. I think of some of the good or meaningful times I have had with the people close to me, to see if they would make good happy memories. Meeting a friend at a railway station on a sunny day seems to have made a good happy memory, even though later we talked about some difficult things, like starvation and dehydration. There were walks in the woods with friends looking for mushrooms that may make happy memories. There have been a few times of gardening together as a family that may make a good happy memory. Working together at some arduous cooking one evening is a happy memory so far. There was a good trip out to a department store. Sitting by the bedside of someone who was dying may actually make a good happy memory. My mother and I once carried a piece of coal on a train to Newcastle together. My mother and I once played cards with some longshoremen on a snowy morning waiting for a ship to come in. There was a time when I lived in a foreign city and returned again and again to a certain botanical garden to look at a certain Cedar of Lebanon, and that is a happy memory, even though I was alone. My neighbor across the street once brought a plate of cake to the back door during a time of mourning. But I can see that if some day she and I were to become estranged, that would spoil the happy memory. I see that happy memories can be erased.

A happy memory can be erased if you do the same thing on another day and you are not happy, for instance if on another day you garden or cook together with bad feeling. I can see that an experience does not make a happy memory if it started out well but ended badly. There is no happy memory if there was something nice about an experience but also some problem, if two of you enjoyed an outing but the third was sitting at home angry because you were so late returning. You have to make sure, somehow, that nothing spoils the thing while it is happening, and then that no later experience erases it. I could have happy memories. I can see that the things I do with another person, and with a feeling of warmth toward that person, and with a person who will want to have me in his or her happy memory may make a good happy memory, while the things I do alone and especially with a feeling of ambition, or pride, or power, even if they are good in themselves, will not make a good happy memory. It is all right to have candy and enjoy it, but I should remember that the memory of candy will not be a happy one. If I am playing a board game with people close to me and we are happy, I must be sure we don't quarrel before the end of it. I must be sure that at some later time we don't play another board game that is unhappy. I should check now and then to make sure I am not alone too much, or unhappy with other people too often. I should add them up, now and then: what are my happy memories so far?

THEY TAKE TURNS USING
A WORD THEY LIKE

"It's *extraordinary*," says one woman.
"It *is* extraordinary," says the other.

MARIE CURIE,
SO HONORABLE WOMAN

PREFACE

Woman of pride, passion, and labor, who was actress of her time because she had the ambition of her means and the means of her ambition, actress of ours, finally, since between Marie and atomic force, the filiation is direct.

Besides, she died of it.

CHARACTER

From birth, Marie possesses the three dispositions that make brilliant subjects, cherished by professors: memory, power of concentration, and appetite for learning.

"My heart breaks when I think of my spoiled aptitudes which, all the same, had to be worth something..."

Then what? The "ordinary destiny of women"? She never imagined making it her own.

IN THE CHALET OF ZAKOPANE

But in the chalet of Zakopane where she lingers, alone, in September 1891, walking her melancholy under the great black pines of the Carpathians, dragging a grippe that does not finish, one man, Casimir, could take her away. And a part of herself hopes.

In two months she will be twenty-four years.

She is poor. She is not yet beautiful. For all diploma she has the Polish baccalaureate. Why would she become "someone"? Besides, she loves Casimir, and waits for him.

Four years have not cooled the sentiments of the young man, probably exalted on the contrary by the obstacle... And he has lost nothing of his charm...

What he does not know, when he mentions their shared future, is that he now has a rival. And what a rival! A laboratory.

Where does she come from, this nervous young woman, who curiously combines timidity and assurance? It is a daughter of the earth, who has need of air, space, trees. She entertains with nature a relationship that is almost carnal. The plants know it and under her fingers blossom.

What she denies, on the other hand, is her animal part. Her brief angers, for example, which betray like a bolt of lightning what she is controlling in the way of concealed storms.

POVERTY

Now, however, her father is deprived of his attributions, loses the lodging that accompanies them and half of his appointments.

How to join the two ends?

He gnaws at himself. Ah!

What afflicts her is not that she has only one dress which

must be made over by a seamstress but that she does not see any way out of the tunnel in which she is engaged.

Then she is rescued by her sister.

STUDIES IN PARIS

French science, whose milk Marie Sklodowska has come to Paris to suck, happily has one great man, Pasteur, who is reaching the end of his life.

In Paris, she will spend her leisure time with her sister Bronia and Bronia's own Casimir. Though they work hard they know how to amuse themselves, with Slavic hospitality. There are infinite discussions around the samovar and the piano in which they remake the world.

They organize parties, put on amateur spectacles, tableaux vivants: a young woman draped in a garnet tunic, her blond hair falling over her shoulders, incarnates Poland breaking its bonds while Paderewski plays Chopin in the wings: it's Marie, proud of having been chosen.

But chatting pleasantly will never be her specialty.

AUSTERITY

Her austerity sometimes borders on masochism. One night she is so cold in her fireless little room that she piles on her bed everything contained in her trunk along with a chair, while the water freezes in her basin.

She sometimes faints from having fed herself exclusively on radishes and tea. Bronia and Casimir rescue her and a cure of beefsteak puts her to rights.

LANGUAGE

A summer passes. She perfects her French. When classes resume, she has driven out all the "Polishisms" from her vocabulary. Only the gently rolled *r's* will bear witness until her last day to her Slavic origins, adding a certain charm to her voice which does not lack it already. And, like all the world, she will always calculate in her mother tongue.

LICENSE

Not only does she pass her exam, but when the results are announced before all the candidates in order of merit, her name is spoken first. Marie Sklodowska is licensed in physical sciences by the University of Paris. And it is admirable.

COURTSHIP

Did she even notice, on the eve of her exam, that Sadi Carnot, the President of the Republic, was stabbed in his carriage by an Italian militant anarchist?

Perhaps she did not speak of it, even for an instant, with the physicist she has been seeing for several weeks, and who, as others offer chocolates, has brought her, when he has come to chat with her in her room, the offprint of an article titled "On symmetry in physical phenomena, the symmetry of an electric field and a magnetic field." The brochure is dedicated "To Mlle Sklodowska with the respect and the friendship of the author P. Curie."

Together they speak enormously, but about physics or themselves.

And, everyone knows, to tolerate a person telling you about his childhood it is necessary to be in love with him.

Previous Loves

Marie has not attained twenty-six years, soon twenty-seven, she has not lived three years in Paris without having met at Bronia's, at the Faculty, at the laboratory, representatives of the male species sensitive to her attractions. An enamored Polish student had once thought to swallow laudanum to make himself interesting in her eyes. Marie's reaction: "That young man has no sense of priorities."

In any case, they did not have the same.

Pierre

Pierre Curie has come on stage in Marie's life at the precise moment at which it was suitable that he should appear.

The year 1894 has begun. Marie is assured of obtaining her license in July. She is beginning to look beyond, she is more available, and the spring is beautiful. Pierre is already captive to this singular little blond person.

It is clear that, making his way at once through the realms of the sublime and of theoretical physics, Pierre still finds himself alone at thirty-five years. And Marie Sklodowska very quickly appears to him as the Unique, capable of accompanying him there.

But lofty thinking is ill compensated. At thirty-six years, Pierre Curie earns thirty-six hundred francs per year at the School of Physics.

Bolt of Lightning

Marie Curie is over fifty years when she writes lines that describs their first meeting and she is never a woman to express herself, publicly at least, like the Portuguese Nun.

But under the convention of the style and the eternal constraint certainly appears a little of what was, it seems, a reciprocal bolt of lightning.

Marie will be perceptibly longer in being convinced that she must alienate her independence, even to this physicist with limpid eyes.

Pierre Curie has said it to her: "Science, is your destiny." Science, that is to say research pursued for practical ends.

Marie tells, in the stilted book she devotes to him: "Pierre Curie wrote me during the summer of 1894 letters which I think admirable taken as a whole."

To one, Pierre adds a postscript: "I have shown your photograph to my brother. Was I wrong? He finds you very good. He says: 'She has a look that is very decided and even stubborn.'"

Stubborn, oh how much!

She, always dressed in gray, gentle yet stern, child-like yet mature, sweet yet uncompromising ... the woman from Poland.

He...

And then they...

DOMESTIC LIFE

The only competition that Pierre has ever accepted and that he has just won, is against Poland.

And thus it is in July 1894 that Marie takes, on the sly, lessons of a new kind with Bronia: how does one make a roast chicken? Fries? How does one feed a husband?

We know, on the other hand, that a cousin has the good idea of sending a check as a wedding present. That the check is exchanged for two bicycles. And that the "little queen," the entirely new invention that became the darling of the French, will be the honeymoon vehicle of M. and Mme Pierre Curie.

The bicycle, is freedom.

RESEARCH

To extract uranium from pitchblende, there are at that time factories. To extract radium from it, there is a woman in a hangar.

She is sure of her method. But her means are derisory.

WORKING WITH RADIUM

Marie gives birth to a daughter, yet does not take time off from work. Why are they so tired, the Curies, when they arrive, with Irene who is cutting her seventh tooth, at Auroux where they have rented a house for the summer?

They struggle to swim in the river and they struggle on their bicycles. And Marie has the tips of her fingers chapped, painful. She does not know, nor Pierre either, that they are beginning to suffer from the irradiation of the radioactive substances they are manipulating.

It is in the following December, on a page of the black notebook not precisely dated and bearing Pierre's writing, that appears for the first time the word *radium*.

What remains is to prove the existence of the new element. "I would like it to have a beautiful color," says Pierre.

Pure salts of radium are colorless, quite simply. But their own radiations color with a blue-mauve tint the glass tubes that contain them. In sufficient quantity, their radiations provoke a visible glow in the darkness.

When that glow begins to irradiate in the darkness of the laboratory, Pierre is happy.

CHILDREN

Marie makes jams and the clothes of her daughters out of a spirit of thrift. Not from zeal.

RELATIONSHIP

When it comes to mathematics, he judges her stronger than he and says it good and loud. She, for her part, admires in her companion "the sureness and the rigor of his reasonings, the surprising suppleness with which he can change the object of his research..."

Each of them has a very high idea of the value of the other.

FELLOW WORKERS

An aura has been created that attracts and impresses at the same time. The echo of their works, the radiance of Pierre, the intensity of Marie, that force which is all the more moving because the young blond woman appears more and more slender under her black smock, the couple they form, the almost religious spirit of their scientific engagement, their asceticism, all this has attracted young researchers in their wake.

A dishevelled chemist, André Debierne, will enter the life of the Curies never to leave it again.

Marie Curie is neither a saint nor a martyr. She is young at a time when most women oscillate between remorse and hysteria, either guilty or "out of their bodies."

GENIUS: RADIOACTIVITY

In fact, two German researchers announce that radioactive substances have physiological effects. Pierre immediately exposes his arm deliberately to a source of radium. With happiness, he sees a lesion form.

To be recognized by their peers—the Curies certainly appreciate that satisfaction. Besides, it is "fair."

Now, it happens that at night she gets up and starts to wander through the sleeping house. Little crises of somnambulism that alarm Pierre. Or it is he who is ravaged by pains that alter his sleep. Marie watches over him, worried, powerless.

And her appearance? Marie is sitting next to Lord Kelvin, in her "formal dress." She has only one, still the same after ten years, black, with a discreet neckline. In truth, it is better that she has no love of toilette, because she has no taste at all and never will have. Black—which distinguishes her, because it is not customary to wear it—and gray to which she has subscribed out of convenience, settle matters well and make a good setting for her ash-blond hair.

FAME

There exists a threshold beyond which disdain for honors borders on affectation, and one would be tempted to think that Marie Curie has crossed it when she complains, in sum, at having received, with Pierre, the Nobel Prize.

Wrested from their bowl, our two goldfish suffocate and thrash about. No, they wish no banquet; no, they wish no tour of America; no, they do not wish to visit the Automobile Show.

However, they are both unconditional admirers of Wagner.

THE DEATH OF PIERRE

He takes the train back from the country Monday evening, carrying a bouquet of ranunculus.

Marie returns Wednesday evening. The rain has resumed in Paris.

The next day, Thursday, Pierre is on his way from his publisher, Gauthier-Villars, to the Institute. The rain has started again. He opens his umbrella. The Rue Dauphine is narrow, congested, he crosses behind a fiacre...

As always, he is absent-minded... Approaching the fiacre in the opposite direction, the driver of a wagon with two horses, coming from the quays and going up the Rue Dauphine, sees appear before his left horse a man in black, an umbrella... The man totters, he tries to seize the horse's harness... Hampered by his umbrella, he has slipped between the two horses which their driver has attempted with all his strength to hold back. But the weight of the heavy wagon, five meters long and loaded with military equipment, drags him forward. It is the back left wheel that crushes Pierre's skull. And now that famous brain, that beloved brain, seeps out on the wet cobblestones...

AT THE POLICE STATION

The body is removed to a police station. An officer picks up his telephone. But Pierre Curie no longer has ears to be annoyed that he belongs, in death as in life, to the number of those for whom one disturbs the Minister of the Interior.

MARIE

Marie remains frozen; then she says: "Pierre is dead? Completely dead?"

Yes, Pierre was completely dead.

REACTION

Telegrams flow in, from all corners of the world, letters pile up, the condolences are royal, republican, scientific, formal, or simply emotional and sincere. Fame and love have been brutally mown down by death...

A new title, a sinister one, is added to those with which Marie has up to then been dubbed. Henceforth she will be called only "the illustrious widow."

Eleven years—that is long. Long enough so that the roots of love, if the tree is robust, plunge so deep that they will subsist always, even dried up.

LETTERS TO PIERRE

She begins to write to Pierre, a sort of laboratory notebook of grief.

"My Pierre, I arise after having slept fairly well, relatively calm. There is scarcely a quarter of an hour of that and here I again want to howl like a wild beast."

Summer is here and the sun, so wounding when in oneself everything is black...

"I spend all my days in the laboratory. I can no longer conceive of anything that can give me personal joy, except perhaps scientific work—but no, because if I were successful, I could not tolerate that you should not know it."

She will be successful. And she will tolerate. Because

that is the law of life.

TEACHING AT THE SORBONNE

As she gives her first lecture, continuing where Pierre left off, something is happening that clouds the eyes, tightens the throats, holds the audience from top to bottom of the tiers of seats frozen with emotion before that little black silhouette.

It was fifteen years ago, to the day, that, arriving from Warsaw, a little Polish student crossed for the first time the courtyard of the Sorbonne. The second life of Marie Curie has begun.

And the chronicler of the *Journal*: "A great victory for feminism... For if woman is admitted to give higher instruction to students of both sexes, where henceforth will be the so-called superiority of the male man? In truth, I tell you: the time is close when women will become human beings."

PROVING THAT RADIUM IS AN ELEMENT BY EXTRACTING THE METAL ITSELF

Marie is the only one to be able to do it. All haloed with that melancholy fame that she bears so soberly, she has touched one heart in particular by the simplicity of her bearing and the precision of the objectives she has fixed for herself: that of Andrew Carnegie.

He decides to finance her research, which he knows how to do with elegance.

In the eyes of the international scientific community, she has become an implacable person, without rival in the domain in which she is an authority, a unique star, because she is a woman, in the constellation that then shines in the sky of science.

Yet "her nerves are ill," as she has been told by some of the doctors participating in the congress. Nerves are never ill. They only say that in some part one is ill.

But in 1910, no one knows that a certain Doctor Freud has already analyzed Dora.

A trip to the Engadine will succeed in restoring her.

SORROW AND HER CHILDREN

Many years will pass before her daughters are old enough so that she can speak with them about what is occupying her days. If she never speaks to them of their father, whose name she has forbidden one to pronounce in her presence, it is that fresh wounds are so prompt to bleed, and since when does one bleed in front of one's children?

To say nothing in order to be sure of controlling herself is her rule, she applies it. This does not facilitate communication.

But she has known the privilege of privileges: coherence.

A SECOND NOBEL PRIZE

At the end of the same year, 1911, it is the jury of the Swedish Academy that gives itself the pleasure of bestowing on her the Nobel Prize. In chemistry this time, and not shared.

But the news reaches her in the heart of a tempest next to which the academic eddies are a spring shower. In a word, due to her association with a certain married man, Langevin, Mme Curie has for a time ceased to be an honorable woman.

CONFLICT WITH THE WORKERS
IN THE LABORATORY

Nor at work are things always smooth. There is a day, for
instance, when the laboratory's head of works is raining
blows on the woman's door and yelling:

"Camel! Camel!"

No doubt she can be.

She is capable of everything.

THE ENTR'ACTE

Thanks to Marthe Klein who has taken her there, she dis-
covers the South of France, its splendor, its August nights in
which one sleeps on the terrace, the warmth of the
Mediterranean where she begins to swim again. Tourists are
rare. Only, on the beach, a few English...

The passion for stones is the only one she is known to
have where ownership is concerned, but this passion is lively: she will also buy a house in Brittany.

She is still slight, slender, supple, walks with bare legs,
in espadrilles, with the manner of a young girl. According
to the days, she carries ten years more or ten years less than
her age.

For some time she has needed glasses, but what could be
more natural?

IN QUEST OF A GRAM OF RADIUM

The courage, the determination, the assurance that made
her the twice-crowned queen of radioactivity are powerless
before the evidence: Paris is a festival, but French science is
anemic. Toward whom, toward what, should she turn?

Those who are most dynamic among the scientists will try to sound the alarm, everywhere, with voice and with pen: whether it be prestige, industrial competition, or social progress, a nation that does not invest in research is a nation that declines.

This, everyone knows more or less—rather less than more—today.

MISSY

And so, one May morning in 1920, Marie welcomes at her office at the Curie Pavillion Henri-Pierre Roché who accompanies a very little graying person with large black eyes, slightly limping: Mrs. Meloney Mattingley, whom her friends call Missy. The minuscule Missy is editor of a feminine magazine of good reputation.

And the unforeseeable is going to happen. One of those mysterious consonances, as frank as a C Major chord. A friendship, whose consequences will be infinite.

Marie is charming, though who knows why, with this bizarre little creature.

IN QUEST OF A GRAM OF RADIUM

Mme Curie is, in a word, poor. In a poor country.

Stupefying! Something to surprise the cottages lining 5th Avenue, certainly.

Missy has a good nature. She loves to admire, and Marie seems to her admirable. This excellent disposition being accompanied by a vigorous practical sense, Missy, who compares herself to a locomotive, moves a series of railway cars if not mountains.

How much does a gram of radium cost? One million

francs, or one hundred thousand dollars. One hundred thousand dollars for a noble cause attached to a grand name— this can be found. Missy believes she can collect it from several very rich compatriots.

She mobilizes the wife of the king of petrol, Mrs. John D. Rockefeller, that of the Vice and future President, Mrs. Calvin Coolidge, and several other ladies of the same caliber.

She takes each bull by the horns—that is, each editor of each New York newspaper by his sentiments.

A Trip to the United States

Evidently, when Missy will have succeeded, Marie will have to come in person to get her gram of radium. In a parallel way, a well-launched autobiography can bring her substantial authors' rights. What benefit will Missy draw personally from the operation? Purely moral.

Correct? Unquestionably.

Friendship

What remains of their correspondence, which is, at times, almost daily, attests to the permanence of the affection that binds these two warriors, equally lame, equally intrepid.

If anyone esteems herself at her true price, it is Marie. If anyone is prepared to pay it, it is Missy. But take care: on both sides, one must be "regular."

Marie has promised to come get her gram of radium herself. Does she confirm? She confirms. To write her autobiography. Does she confirm? She confirms. Good.

The king and queen of Belgium remained six weeks, says Missy. The queen of radium cannot make a less royal visit.

HEALTH

She writes to Bronia: "My eyes are very weakened and probably not much can be done for them. As for my ears, an almost continual buzzing, often very intense, persecutes me. I worry about it very much: my work may be hampered—or even become impossible. Perhaps radium has something to do with my troubles, but one can't declare it with certainty." Radium guilty? It's the first time that she mentions the idea. She will soon have confirmation that she is suffering from a double cataract.

THE TRIP TO AMERICA

Mme Curie is to receive from the hands of the President of the United States the miraculous product of a national collection, one gram of radium.

She shakes hands with a great many people until someone breaks her wrist.

That evening, Missy knows definitively who Marie really is. And reciprocally.

Fabulous razzia: Marie has pocketed in addition fifty thousand dollars advance for her autobiography, though the book is to be insipid. Missy has at every point kept her promises, and well beyond.

LEAVETAKING

The crystalline lenses of the beautiful ash-gray eyes are becoming each day more opaque. She is convinced she will soon be blind. Marie and Missy embrace each other crying.

Let us say right away, however, that these two slender dying creatures will nevertheless meet again. It will be seven years later, again at the White House...

Missy and Marie certainly belong to the same race. That of the irreducibles.

TIME PASSING

And now the red curls of Perrin, discoverer of Brownian motion, have become white.

SCIENTIFIC CONFERENCES

These conferences to which she travels often weigh on her. She finds only one pleasure in them: still a devotee of excursions, she vanishes and goes off to discover a few of the splendors of the Earth. For over fifty years a recluse, she saw almost nothing.

From everywhere, she writes and describes to her daughters. The Southern Cross is "a very beautiful constellation." The Escurial is "very impressive"...The Arab palaces of Grenada are "very lovely"... The Danube is bordered with hills. But the Vistula...Ah! The Vistula! With its most adorable banks of sand, etc. etc.

THE ILLNESS OF MARIE

One afternoon in May 1934, at the laboratory where she has tried to come and work, Marie murmurs: "I have a fever, I'm going home..."

She walks around the garden, examines a rosebush which she herself has planted and which does not look well, asks that it be taken care of immediately... She will not return.

What is wrong with her? Apparently nothing. Yet she has no strength, she is feverish. She is transported to a clin-

ic, then to a sanatorium in the mountains. The fever does not subside. Her lungs are intact. But her temperature rises. She has attained that moment of grace where even Marie Curie no longer wants to see the truth. And the truth is that she is dying.

THE DEATH OF MARIE

She will have a last smile of joy when, consulting for the last time the thermometer she is holding in her little hand, she observes that her temperature has suddenly dropped. But she no longer has the strength to make a note of it, she from whom a number has never escaped being written down. This drop in temperature is the one that announces the end.

And when the doctor comes to give her a shot:

"I don't want it. I want to be left in peace."

It will require another sixteen hours for the heart to cease beating, of this woman who does not want, no, does not want to die. She is sixty-six years old.

Marie Curie-Sklodowska has ended her course.

On her coffin when it has descended into the grave, Bronia and their brother Jozef throw a handful of earth. Earth of Poland.

Thus ends the story of an honorable woman.

Marie, we salute you...

CONCLUSION

She was of those who work one single furrow.

POSTSCRIPT

Nevertheless, the quasi-totality of physicists and mathematicians will refuse fiercely and for a long time to open what Lamprin will call "a new window on eternity."

MIR THE HESSIAN

Mir the Hessian regretted killing his dog, he wept even as he forced its head from its body, yet what had he to eat but the dog? Freezing in the hills, far away from everyone.

Mir the Hessian cursed as he knelt on the rocky ground, cursed his bad luck, cursed his company for being dead, cursed his country for being at war, cursed his countrymen for fighting, and cursed God for allowing it all to happen. Then he started to pray: it was the only thing left to do. Alone, in midwinter.

Mir the Hessian lay curled up among the rocks, his hands between his legs, his chin on his breast, beyond hunger, beyond fear. Abandoned by God.

The wolves had scattered the bones of Mir the Hessian, carried his skull to the edge of the water, left a tarsus on the hill, dragged a femur into the den. After the wolves came the crows, and after the crows the scarab beetles. And after

119

the beetles, another soldier, alone in the hills, far away from everyone. For the war was not yet over.

MY NEIGHBORS
IN A FOREIGN PLACE

Directly across the courtyard from me lives a middle-aged woman, the ringleader of the building. Sometimes she and I open our windows simultaneously and look at each other for an instant in shocked surprise. When this happens, one of us looks up at the sky, as though to see what the weather is going to be, while the other looks down at the courtyard, as though watching for late visitors. Each is really trying to avoid the glance of the other. Then we move back from the windows to wait for a better moment.

Sometimes, however, neither of us is willing to retreat: we lower our eyes and for minutes on end remain standing there, almost close enough to hear each other breathing. I prune the plants in my windowbox as though I were alone in the world and she, with the same air of preoccupation, pinches the tomatoes that sit in a row on her window sill and untangles a sprig of parsley from the bunch that stands yellowing in a jar of water. We are both so quiet that the scratching and fluttering of the pigeons in the eaves above seems very loud. Our hands tremble, and that is the only sign that we are aware of each other.

I know that my neighbor leads an utterly blameless life. She is orderly, consistent, and regular in her habits. Nothing she does would set her apart from any other woman in the building. I have observed her and I know this is true.

She rises early, for example, and airs her bedroom; then, through the half-open shutters, I see what looks like a large white bird diving and soaring in the darkness of her room, and I know it is the quilt that she is throwing over her bed; late in the morning her strong, pale forearm flashes out of the living room window several times and gives a shake to a clean dustrag; in housedress and apron she takes vegetables from her window sill at noon, and soon after I smell a meal being cooked; at two o'clock she pins a dishcloth to the short line outside her kitchen window; and at dusk she closes all the shutters. Every second Sunday she has visitors during the afternoon. This much I know, and the rest is not hard to imagine.

I myself am not at all like her or like anyone else in the building, even though I make persistent efforts to follow their pattern and gain respect. My windows are not clean, and a lacy border of soot has gathered on my window sill; I finish my washing late in the morning and hang it out just before a midday rainstorm breaks, when my neighbor's wash has long since been folded and put away; at nightfall, when I hear the clattering and banging of the shutters on all sides, I cannot bear to close my own, even though I think I should, and instead leave them open to catch the last of the daylight; I disturb the man and woman below me because I walk without pause over my creaking floorboards at midnight, when everyone else is asleep, and I do not carry my pail of garbage down to the courtyard until late at night, when the cans are full: then I look up and see the house-fronts shuttered and bolted as if against an invasion, and only a few lights burning in the houses next door.

I am very much afraid that by now the woman opposite has observed all these things about me, has formed a notion of me that is not at all favorable, and is about to take action with her many friends in the building. Already I have seen them gather in the hallway and have heard their vehement whispers echoing through the stairwell, where they stop every morning on their way in from shopping to lean on the banisters and rest. Already they glance at me with open dis-like and suspicion in their eyes, and any day now they will circulate a petition against me, as my neighbors have done in every building I have ever lived in. Then, I will once again have to look for another place to live, and take some-thing worse than what I now have and in a poorer neigh-borhood, just so as to leave as quickly as possible. I will have to inform the landlord, who will pretend to know nothing about the activity of my neighbors, but who must know what goes on in his buildings, must have received and read the petition. I will have to pack my belongings into boxes once again and hire a van for the day of departure. And as I carry box after box down to the waiting van, as I struggle to open each of the many doors between this apartment and the street, taking care not to scratch the woodwork or break the glass panes, my neighbors will appear one by one to see me off, as they always have. They smile and hold the doors for me. They offer to carry my boxes and show a genuinely kind interest in me, as though all along, given the slightest excuse, they would have liked to be my friends. But at this point, things have gone too far and I cannot turn back, though I would like to. My neighbors would not understand why I had done it, and the wall of hatred would rise between us again.

But sometimes, when this building with its bitter atmosphere becomes too oppressive for me to bear it any longer, I go outside into the city and wander back to the houses I used to live in. I stand in the sun talking to my old neighbors, and I find comfort and relief in their warm welcome.

ORAL HISTORY
(WITH HICCUPS)

My sister died last year leaving two dau   ghters.   My
husband and I have decided to ad   opt the girls. The
older one is thirty-three and a b   uyer for a department
store, and the yo   unger one, who just turned thirty,
works in the st   ate budget office. We have one ch
ild still living at home, and the house is not b   ig, so
it will be a tight fit, but we are willing to do this for their
s   ake. We will move our son, who is eleven, out of his ro
om and into the small room I have been using as a s
ewing room. I will set up my machine d   ownstairs   in
the living room. We will put a bunk bed for the girls in my
s   on's old room. It is a fair-sized room with one cl
oset and one window, and the bathroom is just down the h
all. We will have to ask them not to bring all their th
ings. I assume they will be willing to m   ake that sacri-
fice in order to be part of this family. They will also have to
w   atch what they say at the d   inner table. With
our younger son present we don't want open c
onflict. What I'm worried about is a c   ouple

of pol   itical issues. My older niece is a f   eminist, while my husband and I feel the tables have been turned against m   ales nowadays. Also, my younger niece is probably more pro-g   overnment than either my older niece or my h usband and me. But she will be away a good deal, traveling for her j   ob. And we have d   .   eveloped some negotiating skills with our own ch   ildren, so we should be able to w   ork things out with the two of them. We will try to be firm but f   air, as we always were with our older b   oy before he left h   ome. If we can't w ork things out right away, they can always go to their r oom and c   ool off until they're ready to come back out and be c   ivil. Excuse me.

THE PATIENT

The day after the patient was admitted to the hospital, the young doctor operated on her upper colon, where he felt sure the cause of her illness lay. But his medical training had not been good, the doctors who taught him were careless men, and he had been pushed through school quickly because he was clever and the country was desperate for doctors; the hospital was poorly staffed and the building itself was falling into ruin because of government mismanagement: piles of broken plaster choked the hallways. Because of all this, or for some other reason, the woman's condition did not improve, but grew rapidly worse. The young doctor tried everything. At last he admitted that there was nothing more he could do and that she was on the point of dying. He was overwhelmed by the grief and guilt that come with the first death of a patient. He was at the same time filled with strange excitement, and felt he had joined the ranks of serious men of the world, men who hold the lives of others in their hands and are like gods. Inexplicably, then, the woman did not die. She lay peacefully in a twilight coma. As each

day passed with no change, the young doctor grew more and
more maddened by her immobility. He could not sleep and
his eyes became bloodshot. He had trouble eating and his
face became gaunt. At last he could not contain his frustration any longer. He went to her bedside and drove his fist
again and again into her pinched, yellow face until she did
not look human anymore. One last breath leaked from her
mouth and then, battered and bruised, she died.

RIGHT AND WRONG

She knows she is right, but to say she is right is wrong, in this case. To be correct and say so is wrong, in certain cases.

She may be correct, and she may say so, in certain cases. But if she insists too much, she becomes wrong, so wrong that even her correctness becomes wrong, by association.

It is right to believe in what she thinks is right, but to say what she thinks is right is wrong, in certain cases.

She is right to act on her beliefs, in her life. But she is wrong to report her right actions, in most cases. Then even her right actions become wrong, by association.

If she praises herself, she may be correct in what she says, but her saying it is wrong, in most cases, and thus cancels it, or reverses it, so that although she was for a particular act deserving of praise, she is no longer in general deserving of praise.

ALVIN THE TYPESETTER

Alvin and I worked together typesetting for a weekly newspaper in Brooklyn. We came in every Friday. This was the autumn that Reagan was elected President, and everyone at the newspaper suffered from a sense of foreboding and depression.

The old gray typesetting machines, with their scratches and scars, were set back to back in a tiny room next to the toilet. People raced in and out of the toilet all day long and the sound of flushing was always in our ears. Pinned to the corkboard walls around us as we bent over our keyboards was an ever-thickening forest of paper strips. The damp paper strips were covered with type, and when they had dried, they were taken away by the paste-up people to become columns on the newspaper page.

The work we had to do was not hard, but it required patience and care, and we were under constant pressure to work faster. I typed straight copy, and Alvin set ads. If the machines stopped rumbling for more than a few minutes, the boss would come downstairs to see what was holding us up. And so Alvin and I continued to type while we ate our lunch, and when we talked to each other, as we did from time to time, we talked surreptitiously, sticking our eyes up over the tops of the machines.

We were blue-collar workers. Every time I thought about how we were blue-collar workers, it surprised me, because we were also, with any luck, performing artists. I played the violin. As for Alvin, he was a standup comedian. Every Friday Alvin told me about his career and his life.

For seven months he had auditioned over and over again without success at a well-known club. At last the manager had relented and given him a spot. Every week now he came on in the dead early hours of Sunday morning for five minutes to close the show. Sometimes the audience liked him and sometimes it did not respond at all. If the manager occasionally left him on stage for ten minutes or gave him a spot earlier in the evening, at 9:30, Alvin felt this was an important advance in his career.

Alvin could not describe his art except to say that he had no script, no routine, that he never knew just what would happen on stage, and that this lack of preparation was part of his act. From the snatches of monologue he spoke for me, however, I could see that some of his patter was about sex—he made jokes about cream and sperm—and that some of his patter was about politics, and that he also liked to do impersonations.

He usually worked without any props. In the week of Election Day, in November, he carried to the nightclub a special patriotic kerchief covered with red, white, and blue American symbols to wear over his head. Most often, though, what he took out on stage was only himself, as though his long, solemn face were a mask, or his body a marionette that he controlled with strings from above, slim, loose-joined, floating over the floor. He had his stance, his silences, his bald head, and his clothes. He wore the same clothes on stage that he wore to work: dark formal pants and often a shirt of cheap synthetic material covered with palm trees or pine trees on a white background.

When I arrived at the office, Alvin would be typing at his machine in his stocking feet, and his long narrow shoes would be sitting next to my machine. If Alvin was glum, neither of us said much. If he was elated, he could not help standing up from his machine and talking. And on some days I would speak to him and he would look at me blankly. He would later admit that he had been smoking hash for days on end.

Over the clicking of the machines Alvin told me that he lived apart from his wife and son. His son did not like Alvin's friends or the food Alvin ate, and made the same excuse over and over again not to see him. He told me about his circle of friends—a group of Brooklyn vegetarians. He was planning to eat Thanksgiving dinner with these vegetarians and he was planning to spend the Christmas holiday sleeping at the YMCA. He told me about his travels—to Boston and places in New Jersey. He asked me many times to go out on a date with him. We went once to the circus.

He told me about the typesetters' agency that never found him any work. "Don't I seem ambitious to you?" he asked. He complained to me about the lack of order in our office, and about the poor writing in the pieces we were given to typeset. He said it was not part of his job to correct spelling and grammar. He told me with indignation that he would not do more than should be expected of him. He and I had a sense of our superiority to those in charge of us, and this was only aggravated by the fact that we were so often treated as though we had no education.

Because Alvin was good-natured and presented himself to the rest of the newspaper staff without reservation, because his whole art consisted of isolating and exposing himself as a figure of fun, he was well liked by many of them but also became a natural victim of some: the manager of the production department, for instance, kept pushing him to work faster and often asked him to do his ads over again, and talked against Alvin behind his back. Alvin responded to this goading with injured pride. But worse than the production manager was the owner of the paper, who worked most of the week upstairs in his office but on press day came down to the production department and sat on a stool alongside the others.

He was a little man with a red mustache and glasses who wore his flannel shirts tucked into his bluejeans and smelled of deodorant when he became excited. He never walked slowly and he was in and out of the toilet faster than anyone else: no sooner had the door shut behind him than we would hear the thunderous flush from the tank overhead and he would spring out the door again. For much of the week he talked to his employees with good humor, though not to us, the typesetters, and tolerated the caricatures of his face posted all over the room and the remarks about him written on the toilet wall. On press day, however, and when things were going badly at the paper, his sense of catastrophe would drive him to turn on us one by one and dress us down publicly in a way that was humiliating and surrounded by silence. What made this treatment especially hard to accept was that our pay was low and our paychecks bounced regularly. The accountant upstairs could not keep track of where the newspaper's money was, and she added on her fingers.

Alvin received the worst of it and hardly defended himself at all: "I thought you said... I thought they told me to... I thought I was supposed to..." Any answer he made provoked another outburst from the boss, until Alvin retired in silence. I was embarrassed by his lack of pride. He was afraid of losing his job. But after Christmas his attitude changed.

Over the holidays, Alvin and I both performed. I played the violin in a concert of excerpts from "The Messiah." Alvin's performance was to be an entire evening of monologues and songs at a local club run by a friend. Before the event Alvin handed out a Xeroxed flyer with crooked lettering and a picture of himself wearing a beret. In his text he called himself "the widely acclaimed." The tickets were five dollars. Our newspaper ran an ad for his performance and everyone who worked with us there showed great interest in the event, though when the evening came, no one from the newspaper actually went to see him.

When Alvin came in to work on the Friday following his performance, he was the center of attention for a few minutes and an aura of celebrity floated around him. But Alvin told a sad tale. There were only five people in the audience at his performance. Four were fellow comedians, and the fifth was Alvin's friend Ira, who talked throughout his monologues.

Alvin was eloquent about his failure. He described the room, his friend the owner, his friend Ira. He talked for five minutes. The boss, who had been listening with the others, grew restless and distracted and told Alvin there was work waiting for him. Alvin raised a hand in concession and went into the typesetting room. The production people returned to their stools and bent over their pages. Our machines began rumbling. The boss hurried upstairs.

Then Alvin stopped typing. His pupils were dilated and he looked particularly remote. He stood up and walked out. He said to the production room at large: "Listen: I have work to do. But I haven't started yet. I would like to perform for you first."

Most of the production people smiled because they liked Alvin.

"Now I'm going to impersonate a chicken," he said.

He climbed up on a stool and started flapping his arms and clucking. The room was quiet. The production people perched on their long-legged stools like a flock of resting egrets and stared at this bald chicken. When there was no applause, Alvin shrugged and climbed down and said, "Now I'm going to impersonate a duck," and waddled across the room with his knees bent and toes turned in. The production people glanced around the room at one another. Their looks darted and hopped like sparrows. They gave Alvin a spattering of applause. Then he said, "Now I'm going to do a pigeon." He shook his shoulders and jerked his head forward and back as he strutted in the circular patterns of a courting pigeon. He managed to convey something of the ostentation of a male pigeon. Abruptly he stopped and said to his audience, "Well, don't you have any work to do? What are you sitting around for? All this should have been done yesterday!" The little hair he had was poking straight out from his head as though he were full of electricity. He swallowed his saliva. "That's all we are," he said. "A bunch of dumb birds."

The smiles faded from the faces of his audience. The weariness of that leafless late December, our fear of our weakened government, our dread of its repressive spirit, descended on us once again.

Into the abrupt silence came the chiming of a church-bell across the street. The production manager by reflex checked his watch. Alvin's body sagged. He turned and walked into our tiny room. The back of his head had its own expression of defeat.

For a moment everyone stared at him in amazement. He sat slumped over his machine, solitary, flooded by fluorescent light, exhausted by his performance. He had not been very funny, in fact he was a poor actor, and yet something about his act had been impressive: his grim determination, the violence of his feelings. One by one the production people went back to work: paper rustled, scissors clattered on the stone tabletop, murmurs passed back and forth over the sound of the radio. I sat down at my machine and Alvin looked up at me from under his heavy lids. His look carried all the hurt, the humiliation, the mockery of the past few months. He said without smiling, "They think I'm nothing. They can think what they like. I have my plans."

SPECIAL

We know we are very special. Yet we keep trying to find out in what way: not this way, not that way, then what way?

SELFISH

The useful thing about being a selfish person is that when your children get hurt you don't mind so much because you yourself are all right. But it won't work if you are just a little selfish. You must be very selfish. This is the way it happens. If you are just a little selfish, you take some trouble over them, you pay some attention to them, they have clean clothes most of the time, a fresh haircut fairly often, though not all the supplies they need for school, or not when they need them; you enjoy them, you laugh at their jokes, though you have little patience when they are naughty, they annoy you when you have work to do, and when they are very naughty you become very angry; you understand some of what they should have, in their lives, you know some of what they are doing, with their friends, you ask questions, though not very many, and not beyond a certain point, because there is so little time; then the trouble begins and you don't notice signs of it because you are so busy: they steal, and you wonder how that thing came into the house; they show you what they have stolen, and when you ask questions, they lie;

when they lie, you believe them, every time, because they seem so candid and it would take so long to find out the truth. Well, if you have been selfish, this is what sometimes happens, and if you have not been selfish enough, then later, when they are in serious trouble, you will suffer, though even as you suffer you will continue, from long habit, to be selfish, saying, I am so distraught, My life has ended, How can I go on? So if you are going to be selfish at all, you must be more selfish than that, so selfish that although you are sorry they're in trouble, sincerely and deeply sorry, as you will tell your friends and acquaintances and the rest of the family, you will be privately relieved, glad, even delighted, that it isn't happening to you.

MY HUSBAND AND I

My husband and I are Siamese twins. We are joined at the forehead. Our mother feeds us. When we are moved to copulate we join lower down as well forming a loop like a certain espaliered tree. Time passes. I separate from my husband below and give birth to twins who are not joined together as we are. They squirm on the ground. Our mother cares for them. They are most often asymmetrical with each other, even in sleep when they lie still. Awake, they stay near each other, as though elastic bands held them, and near us and near our mother. At night the bond is even stronger and we snap together and lie in a heap, my husband's hard muscles against my soft muscles, against our mother's stringy old muscles, and our babies' feather muscles, our arms around one another like so many snakes, and distant thumping music in the fields behind us.

SPRING SPLEEN

I am happy the leaves are growing large so quickly.

Soon they will hide the neighbor and her screaming child.

HER DAMAGE

On the counter lay a pile of plastic packets of duck sauce, soy sauce, and mustard from their Chinese dinner. In her anger she was provoked by the smooth, slippery little bodies and slammed her fist down among them. Two or three exploded. She could not see through her tears. Her bathrobe cuff was drenched in mustard, and the next morning he discovered a spatter of soy sauce, or maybe duck sauce, over the ceiling, two windows, and one wall. She cleaned it off the windows, but it wouldn't come off the ceiling, where it had stained through the white paint, and then when she was done trying to get it off she saw that the drops of detergent and water falling on the wood floor had spotted the finish.

A few days later, carrying the baby, she stepped into a hole in the dining room floor in the old house where a plank had been removed because of termites. She bruised her arm badly, though the baby was not hurt. Then she stopped up the coffee maker with coffee grounds so that it overflowed onto the counter and floor when it went on in the morning. She sprayed the side of her face with the spray attachment at the sink. She burned her hand feeding the wood stove. The baby rolled off the side of their bed and fell onto the floor. She took the baby out for a walk late in the afternoon when the temperature was below freezing, its face turned red, and it started screaming with pain. This was the holiday season.

They sat talking peacefully before dinner. He said she probably needed to get more sleep. She was waiting for the oven to heat, but had forgotten to turn it on.

At dinner, he pointed out that the soy sauce had also spotted the apples in the fruit bowl and the lamp over the dining table. He went on to remind her of the toilet seat she had broken. It was an expensive red Swedish toilet seat. The lid had slipped out of her hand and dropped, cracking the seat. He had immediately taken the whole thing off and replaced it with a green one.

He had also replaced the plastic sheeting over the door to the deck because it had shattered when she left the door open in the cold. Then for the second time she disengaged the connection of a wire over the bedroom door. As he stood on a chair fixing it, she asked him if she could hold the light for him, but he said No, just don't slam the door anymore when you get mad.

The most recent thing was that she took a roll of photographs with no film in the camera, though this did not cost them any money or cause any damage, except for the baby's weariness in its many poses and her regret for the lost pictures, so many of which she remembered clearly, the last being a shot of an oil barge with a tugboat coming up the creek through the first winter ice toward her where she stood at the window, beginning to realize there was no film in the camera.

WORKING MEN

Now that we are living out here in the country the only people we see are working men who come to do jobs for us. They are independent and self-reliant, and they start work early in the day and they work hard without stopping. Last week it was Bill Bray, to install the washing machine. Next week it will be Jay Knickerbocker, to tear off the front of the porch. Today it is Tom Tatt. Tom Tatt is supposed to come disconnect some wires for us. Where is he? Early in the morning we stand in the kitchen together. Where is Tom Tatt? We walk outdoors. Here in the early sunshine is Tom Tatt. He has already finished the job, and is snubbing the cut ends of wire with little black snubs.

IN A NORTHERN COUNTRY

Magin was over seventy and not well. His right leg was lame and his lungs were weak. If his wife had been alive, she would not have let him go. As it was, his friends had told him to stay at home and wait for his brother Michael to come back. Yet he had never listened to anyone but his wife, and now he did not listen to anyone.

He was close to Silit, if the maps of the Trsk Land Office were correct. He had walked since early morning, very slowly, and his feet were sore. Just at noon, he came within sight of the town. His brother's postcard had been sent from here. Karsovy, therefore, should be only a few miles to the north.

He set down his bag on the snow and rubbed his cramped fingers. He looked up at Silit: the street was lined by narrow houses with shuttered windows. Many of the roofs had fallen in and tumbled over the doorsills. Down by the well at the end of the street, under a couple of pine trees, he saw two old women knitting on a bench. He picked up his bag and walked to them and they stopped knitting to stare at him.

Until he shouted his question, they did not understand him. Then one of them opened her mouth and pointed wordlessly across the street.

In the shadow of the eaves, a man sat combing his brown beard with a broken comb. His eyes were on Magin. A roofless car was parked in the lane beside him.

Magin crossed the street. "Can you take me to Karsovy?" he asked in Trsk. The man stopped moving.

"There's no such place," he said.

"There must be," said Magin. He pulled out the creased postcard from his brother and started to thrust it at the man.

"There is not. You are mistaken."

Magin dropped his bag and shook his fist in the man's face, crumpling the postcard. He would not argue. "I am not mistaken," he shouted. His voice broke.

The man was startled. "Well," he said, spitting on his palm and rubbing his boot with it, "I don't often go there."

Magin was trembling with anger and the blood at his temples throbbed. "How much?" he asked.

"I'll take fifty," the man said. Magin drew a purse from his back pocket and laid two coins on the man's palm.

Magin picked up his bag and followed the man to the car. The man pulled himself up into the driver's seat, looking straight ahead. Magin hoisted his bag onto the back seat and climbed in beside it. When he sat down, the springs gave way so far that he came to rest on something that felt like an iron rod. He did not move.

The engine turned over and the car jerked forward and threw Magin against the back of the seat. The car skidded into the snowy ruts of the road. Magin lurched from side to side as the trees veered at him around the bends of the road. Two doves flapped away as the car passed them

The driver's hostility bewildered Magin. As an hour passed in the monotonous woods, he grew more and more uneasy. His search might be hopeless. There had been no word from his brother for weeks. And there was the question of how long he himself would last. "This is crazy," he said to himself suddenly. "Here I am with one foot in the grave, in a north country winter, and I expect something to come of it. Mary would have laughed." He pulled the collar of his overcoat up around his chin.

At last they reached Karsovy. As they drew up into a large clearing, Magin saw women in black crossing the drifts like shadows. Men crouched in front of their doorways.

Magin climbed down with his bag and rested against the car door. He looked up and saw that several people had gathered and were watching him. The women inched forward: their eyes flew from his face to his bag, but not a word passed their lips. Magin searched among the stony-faced men for the leader of the village, and the people became uneasy. They were puzzled by him.

"What?" said Magin to the driver, who had not moved from his seat. "What are they waiting for? Why are they staring at me? Why don't they say anything?"

"Why should they say anything?" the driver said finally. "Anyway, you wouldn't understand them. No one understands them. They don't even know how to speak Trsk." He smacked the wheel. "I brought another old man like you out this way. That was months ago and no one's heard of him since." He spat in the snow and glanced at the villagers with contempt. Before Magin could speak, he leaned on the horn, turned the car, and drove back into the woods.

Magin wondered what to do. One by one the villagers turned and went away, glancing back over their shoulders and stopping in mid-step to stare at him again. Two women stayed behind. One was old, thin, and shabbily dressed. The other was younger, and more muscular. The old one started forward, tightening her kerchief and opening her toothless mouth in a smile. The other one caught her by the sleeve.

"Ninininini," the old one said, her tongue against the roof of her mouth, and her eyes glimmered from under the brow of her kerchief. She pulled away from the younger one and started forward again. The younger one cuffed her lightly on the shoulder and hissed at her. The old one turned and spat, and then walked away, her skirt trailing over the snow behind her.

The younger woman motioned to Magin to follow her. They turned up a small path, Magin favoring one leg. Under the trees he felt the cold close in on him like a vise. He coughed. His breath rattled in his throat.

The path wound among the stone huts. Heavily-furred dogs lay before many of the doors and growled as Magin and the woman went by. At the end of the path lay the woman's hut. With one hand on the latch, she took a quick look back at Magin. Standing next to her, he caught a whiff of her fetid clothes. She opened the door and Magin followed her blindly. He was assaulted by the smell of unwashed linen. Slowly the air came in from the outside and he breathed more easily.

When his eyes grew accustomed to the pale light that

fell over the back of the room from the small windows and the chinks in the stone, he saw that the hut was divided into two rooms by a thin wooden wall. To his left, in the larger room, he made out a table, a cupboard, some chairs, a bed, and on the far wall a framed photograph of the country's leader in military dress. To his right was a small room, doorless. He could see the end of a narrow cot, and nothing else. The woman, standing close beside him, pushed on his shoulder.

"Ehh, ehh," she said, and nodded. He went into the little room and dropped his bag by the bed. He was so tired that he could hardly bear the weight of his clothes. He wanted to lie down, but he was embarrassed by the woman behind him.

He looked out the window and then turned around. The woman had left. He lay down and closed his eyes tightly. He could not even remember why he was here. He began dreaming before he was fully asleep. He dreamt of the train ride through France, though that was already several days behind him. His wife, her hair slipping from its pins with the motion of the train, was reading aloud to him from a newspaper, like a child in her outmoded glasses and ill fitting dress. Yet in the dream he felt that he was the one in the wrong place.

Less than two hours later, waking from his sleep, he saw his brother's tape recorder on a shelf in the corner of the room. He waited for this vision to fade.

It often happened, now, that his memory failed or that he recreated things he remembered and placed them where they did not actually exist.

The tape recorder remained, however, and beside it he now saw a neat pile of notebooks, some clothing, a sewing box, a pair of slippers, a pair of boots, and a knife. Was it possible that his brother had lived in this room? Magin did not move, for fear his brother's possessions would vanish.

After fifteen minutes or so, Magin was fully awake. He got up and went over to the shelf. Touching his brother's possessions, he felt reassured. This was his brother's room: he had often been in his brother's room when his brother was absent, though this was a different room from any of the others. Yet this was his brother's room, and that meant that though his brother was now gone from the room, he would return to it.

And yet why, in that case, had the woman allowed him to lie down and go to sleep here? Perhaps she had merely been showing him the room, and did not intend him to sleep here. Or perhaps she thought he would wait for his brother here. And, after all, that was what he was actually doing, now.

But there was a musty, disused smell about the clothes. And the notebooks stuck together, so that when Magin touched one, they all moved in a block. Perhaps his brother had been gone for a long time. He could not be dead, because in that case the woman would have put his possessions away somewhere. Unless this was where she had put them.

When he went out of the room, the woman was setting a meal on the table. Magin took her arm and led her into the small room. He pointed to his brother's possession and asked her, "Where is the man who owns these things?"

She answered him only by gesturing toward the objects on the shelf in a way which Magin could not understand. She said one or two words only, and these he could not identify in any way with Trsk. Though this disappointed him, it did not surprise him. His brother had come here in order to record the language, after all. He had said it was on the point of dying out.

Magin gave up, not knowing what move to make, and followed the woman back to the table. Out the window, there were long violet shadows under the trees. He sat down, very hungry. He looked at the food. A cube of dry meat stood next to a heel of bread. He could see that the meat was too tough for his old teeth. He picked up the bread and ate it little by little, letting it soften before he chewed it. His hunger faded.

As the woman cleared the table, Magin lit a thin, cheap cigar and immediately started to cough. He felt a certain satisfaction in having come this far. However, he did not see how he was going to find out where his brother was: he was rather helpless, it turned out, because of the language. He stubbed his cigar and slipped what remained of it back in its box.

The woman put on her overcoat and gestured toward the door. Magin thought, with sudden hope, that now she was going to show him how to find Michael. In his excitement, he forgot where his room was, and stood still until the woman pushed him in the right direction. He put on his coat and followed her.

Outside the hut, the birds were now quiet; there was almost no light left in the sky, and the air was sharp.

Magin, hurrying, stumbled over hidden roots. The dogs were gone from the doorways of the huts, which he and the woman passed quickly. When Magin thought they were still far away from the clearing, the sky widened. The windows of the largest hut glowed with orange firelight. Magin's mouth was dry. He swallowed and walked after the woman into the hut.

Before he could steady himself, the woman disappeared from his side. At first the firelight dazzled him. He looked down. A dog was snaking toward him with its belly to the ground. The room was dense with people. In perfect silence they watched him: near the fire, men squatted on low stools and benches digging rhythmically into the thick socks that covered their ankles and scratching their scalps and ears; farther away, in a disordered group, the women sat together hissing over their needlework, shrugging fitfully, and sucking their teeth.

The dog began snarling, and the silence exploded: a tall man with a hooked nose rushed toward the dog, who was crouching at Magin's feet with its teeth bared. A bench tumbled to the floor. The man kicked the dog in the ribs. The dog yelped and slipped away through legs and under stools. The men by the fire roared, and the women cried out strangely, themselves like animals. The dog squirmed into a corner. The man looked at Magin.

In Trsk, Magin said, "I came up here to look for my brother Michael, a scholar. My brother Michael came here to study your language." He stopped because the man obviously did not understand him and was turning away. The man looked among the women for the one who had brought

Magin here, and pointed at her, pronouncing what to Magin was only a guttural noise. The woman rose and spoke long enough to explain everything she knew. The man took Magin by the sleeve and sat him down on a bench near the fire. He spoke to an old man who was bent over a checkerboard in one corner of the room, and then went away. The man had not responded.

Magin lit the butt of his cigar and sat still for some time, wondering what was going to happen. The women sewed placidly, murmuring to one another. The men passed a jug around. For Magin, they poured the liquor into an earthenware cup. They scratched and talked, smiling and nodding at Magin every so often. Occasionally a man would come to him and recite a few words in English, which startled Magin extremely. "No, no. Sky," one would say. Or another would say, "No, yes, here. Tape two."

Magin threw the end of his cigar into the fire and kept an eye on the old man in the corner. The game was nearing its end. The long white hair of the old man grazed the scabbed pate of his opponent whenever they leaned over the board. Every time the white-haired one moved a piece, the other screwed up his nut-like face in anger. Magin lit another cigar and coughed. He was so tired that he could hardly sit straight. Suddenly the bald old man was on his feet, his skull gleaming in the firelight.

"Ruckuck," he cried and brought his fist down on the checkerboard. The pieces—red and black discs and a few fragments of stone and wood—flew through the air and fell on the floor like a shower of hail. The white-haired man smiled calmly, his nose nearly touching his chin.

Now at last he looked at Magin and reluctantly came and sat down beside him. Magin stubbed out his cigar and put the end back in the box.

"Seek old man?" asked the white-haired man in Trsk.

"I'm looking for my brother," said Magin.

"Brother here," said the man.

Magin became excited. "Here?" He pointed to the ground.

"No, no, no." The man held up his hand impatiently. "Brother here. Then: brother gone. Brother gone with man—north. Lost. Gone, lost. Gone, dead. Maybe." He sliced his throat with one finger.

"What man?" Magin asked.

"Leader, cousin." The man pointed to himself. "Gone to hunt." He made the motion of shooting a rifle.

"How long?" Magin asked. He was lighting the butt of his cigar, though he did not know it. The people were all quiet, though they could not understand anything.

"Gone two day, two night. Then very cold, snow fall. Gone five week." He held up his hand, fingers spread. He pointed to himself. "I leader, soon." He smiled.

Magin started coughing and the old man left to get a drink. Magin could not catch his breath, and his eyes watered. Then he began to cry without control. He had drunk too much.

Later, the women put away their work and pulled on their coats and shawls by the light of a few stuttering candles. The men knocked the ashes from their pipes, smacked each other across the back and walked to the door. The women followed. When they had all gone, Magin sat for a

155

few minutes in the dark and smelly room, trying to collect his thoughts. It was not easy. He believed, for some time, that he was in the Smoking Room of the Engineers Club. He was waiting for Harry to come out of the cloakroom. His head swam. He remembered where he was and got up hastily, afraid of losing track again.

Outside he looked over the dim snow to the trees. He did not remember which direction to take. He searched for something familiar in the dark landscape. Hearing a faint noise, he turned and saw small shadows moving over the snow. The first to reach him was a thin, white dog, who paused and stiffened, its nose pointed up at him. It was joined by a larger dog, who walked with difficulty and whose stomach was distended, stretching its worn black skin like a drum. One by one they came up, until a small pack had formed around him. He had nothing to offer them. He leaned down and smoothed the white dog's head. The bones of the skull were round under his palm. The dog did not move. Fearing the sudden snarl and bite, Magin drew back his hand and walked cautiously away. His heart was jolting. He saw a twisted pine tree at the edge of the open space, and recognized it. Near it he found the path.

The dogs walked a few feet behind him, their footsteps muffled by the snow. He was uncomfortable. When the hut came in sight, a dog growled behind him. As he turned, the white dog caught his pants legs between its teeth. The dog growled again and shook its head from side to side. The cloth ripped and Magin began running. His old legs did not move very fast. The dogs dashed back and forth and snapped at his ankles. He reached the hut. As he struggled with the latch, they fell back. Once inside, he stopped to catch his breath, which was raking his throat. Out the window, he saw the dogs circle among themselves, sniff at his footprints, and settle on their haunches, watching the door. Magin went to his cot and lit a fresh cigar. He sat down without undressing and smoked, trying to remain calm. Stubbing his cigar on the dirt floor, he wrapped himself in a thin blanket and lay back. He fell asleep only after a long time.

Most of the night, the cold kept waking him. Toward morning, he slept deeply at last, then lightly again, dreaming of pains in his chest. The dreams became more and more vivid until his eyes were open on a window of pink light and he knew that the violence in his left lung was not a dream. He could not leave the bed. He wanted to smoke, but did not dare. Lying still, staring straight up, he struggled with the pain, resisting every attack, and relaxing when the pain died.

Curiously, what he had learned the night before seemed less final in the daylight. The village leader was gone, with his brother. The people were choosing a new village leader, supposing that the other was dead. They supposed that his brother was dead too. Yet there were other possibilities: his brother might be ill, or injured; someone might be caring for him in a place where there was no way of sending word. Yet the thought haunted Magin that he might have made a foolish decision in coming, and that he could not escape the consequences. He tried to draw a breath and the pain stopped him. Fighting the pain, he then saw that he had had no choice. He could not have stayed at home. There was nothing for him at home. Everything, now, was where his brother was. The pain slowly diminished. After half an hour, as the room grew more and more yellow with the rising sun, Magin was able to sit up.

His wrinkled and sticky clothes clung to him. He had not taken them off since leaving the river three days before. He reached under the bed for his bag and opened it. Inside was a pile of fresh linen. He shut the bag again. He found a safety pin in his pocket and pinned together the bottom of his pants leg. He breathed in his own musty smell. He ran his fingers through his hair and stood up. The pain had perceptibly weakened him and his knees trembled as he walked into the other room.

The dogs were gone. The tracks in front of the door startled the woman. Magin pointed to his torn pants and tried to tell her what had happened. She took an old twig broom and swept away the tracks. The snow against the trees was stained yellow.

At breakfast, Magin ate even less bread than he had the night before. He craved coffee, but sipped cold tea. He lit a cigar and kept it between his fingers without daring to smoke it. Then he walked outdoors, leaving his overcoat behind. Blinking in the glare of the sunlight, he shaded his eyes, which were pale and sensitive. From among the trees he heard men's voices rise and break off. Birds twittered without pause, chipping away at the silence between the trees. He walked along the path, and the ground under his feet was smooth.

He reached the edge of the clearing in time to see two men struggling out of the underbrush on the opposite side,

dragging behind them the corpse of a large deer that fur-
rowed and reddened the snow. His throat tightened as he
watched them slit the deer's belly and disembowel it. Dogs
crouched on their haunches at a small distance, ready to
spring forward. Women carried up pans and buckets to
catch the blood and innards. A few other men gathered
around the animal, and fingered its antlers and hefted its
limbs. Magin went up to them and they turned their heads
and smiled at him. The brown body was stretched out on
the snow, its neck arched and its belly caved in. It was a
young buck. The smallest man grabbed Magin's wrist with
a soft, wet hand and pulled him over to feel the antlers.
They were downy, and warm from the sun. Magin studied
them and the pain began to grow again in his lung. The tall
man with the hooked nose came up with a saw in his fist,
and Magin moved back. The man kneeled to saw off the
antlers. A thin stream of dust fell onto the snow. Magin
grew dizzy as he watched them under the hot sun. His knees
gave way and two men caught him and held him up. The
man with the hooked nose let fall the deer's head, round and
bare, and stood up with the antlers in one hand and the saw
in the other. Magin sat down on a large rock.

A few men had lit a fire on the ground and were roast-
ing the innards over it. The flames were hardly visible in the
noon sun. Near the woods, the dogs fought over the deer's
stomach and intestines. The old man came up to Magin's
rock with a charred stick in his hand. On the end of the
stick was one of the deer's kidneys. He sat down beside
Magin, cut off a piece of kidney with a blunt knife, and held
it out to Magin with his thumb clamped across it.

"Eat," he said in Trsk.

Magin took the meat, unwillingly, and ate it, though it sickened him. He wiped his fingers on the snow and dried them on his pants. The other men swallowed their meat as quickly as the dogs, stood up sleepily, and began to cut the deer into pieces.

The pain continued to grow in Magin's chest. When it gave him a moment of respite, he asked the old man beside him, "What do you think I should do?"

The old man chewed steadily, looking away. When he answered, the pain had attacked Magin again and he could not hear him. When it stopped, he put his hand on the old man's arm. The old man pushed his meat into his cheek and said, "Wait, wait. Later will be news." He shifted the bolus of meat around with his tongue. "One month, two months."

Magin sat still in disappointment. The old man beside him swallowed his meat and fell into a doze. Magin then lit the stub of cigar which had gone out as he held it. With his first lungfull of smoke, the pain became severe and he started coughing. The mucus in his handkerchief was pink. He became aware that he was quite sick. It did not occur to him that he might not leave with his brother, or that he might not leave at all. He had always been able to leave a place, and his brother had always been alive and in a place known to Magin. Only Magin's wife was gone when he expected her to remain.

When, later, the sound of a shotgun from deep in the woods roused him from his thoughts, there was a wide plate of shadow across the clearing. He had not noticed the old man leave. He was cold, but did not know it until he saw that his hands were as blue as the shadows on the snow. The air was sharp in his throat and he had very little strength left in his legs as he went up the path. He stopped now and then to rest. When he was nearly to the hut, he heard a thrashing in the brush nearby. Looking through the trees, he saw a doe on the ground. Her body was steaming in the air. In the snow under her heaving side, a large hole was opening where the blood from her wound melted it. Her eyes were moist. Curious, Magin left the path and pushed through the snow and branches to where she lay.

She was still. Only her eyelids moved. But when Magin came near her, she thrashed again, digging her hind legs into the brush and lunging forward with her head. The blood spurted from her side. Then she lay still again, panting, and Magin leaned over her, pitying her. Without warning, her hind leg drew back, trembling, and shot out, striking him in the ribs.

Magin fell backward into the snow, and was only half conscious of what had happened to him. The snow seeped through his hair.

After a long time, dim forms drew near him, circling around him. Hot breath washed over his ear and cheek, and the harsh stink of malnourished animals filled his nostrils. Then there were voices of men, and snarling and yelping. Someone moved him and the pain sharpened until he lost consciousness.

He woke late at night in his bed, remembering nothing. His body, sheathed in blankets, struggled against fever. Pain sat like a rock in his chest. The pillow was hard under his head and his bones ached. When he shivered in the heat, his skin prickled and stung under his damp clothes. His swollen eyes were dry in their sockets, and his chest labored for air. He fought against this weariness, afraid that if he slept, he would stop breathing. But his weariness overcame him little by little. The fever spread. His limbs shook until the bedframe itself trembled, and sweat ran from him until the mattress under him was damp.

A white snowfield blinded him. A cold north wind crossed it, opening small holes in the ground and leaving banks of steam in its wake. Out of the holes crawled many deer, no larger than mice. Blinking feebly in the light, they tapped the snow with their hooves. As one of them drew its body up out of a hole, a dog leaped on it and devoured it with a convulsive jerking motion. Magin ran at the dog to beat it off, and caught his foot in a hole. He fell forward, his sight clouded by the steam. The cold crept into his bones, and he shivered uncontrollably. In the gloaming that filled the room he groped for some covering. The blanket burned under his hand. He barely had the strength to grasp it and draw it up over his body.

His eyes rested on the pale window. A late rising moon shone over the sill, casting a gray light on the floor. The rotten floorboards softened and began to cave in. As the wood crumbled, Magin saw, down in the darkness under the house, the face of a light-haired man. Magin saw that his skin was steely gray and mottled, as though he had been there a long time. Magin watched, and the dead man moved restlessly, then opened his eyes.

Magin woke, his heart thumping. He saw the large circle of the sun outside his window. Turning his face, looking for darkness, he saw, without recognizing her, the woman standing in the doorway. She backed away from him. Shadows moved in the hut. He smelled fear.

"Don't go," he said. From beyond the wall, whispered echoes of his words came back to confuse him.

"I'm here," he said.

The echoes died. White faces with hollow eyes passed his doorway, curious. Slender hands pointed to the pit in the floor and the stiff, ivory face of the man. The sun grew hotter, singeing the wool of the blankets and suffocating him. Trying to free himself of the tangled blankets, he ripped his clothes and meshed his fingers in the tattered cloth. Groaning, he scratched at his own skin, trying to find a way out of his fevered body. The sun dimmed, leaving him exhausted. He slept deeply without dreaming.

When he opened his eyes, the room was again black. He heard the sound of the woman snoring. He was thirsty. "Wake up," he said. His voice was too feeble. He drew a shallow breath and as the pain increased, spoke again. He coughed and choked on his mucus. The woman only shifted in her bed. He lay back to wait for dawn to draw her from her sleep. Slowly he worked the blankets off his burning legs. A cool breeze blew over his skin.

In the morning, the pain had climbed into his throat, so that he could not swallow without tears coming to his eyes. As though mocking his own darkness, the sun shone over the bed where his limbs gleamed through the rents in this clothes. He looked at his body and saw that it was wasted: the veins stood out over his arms where the flesh had shrunk, and his skin was like parchment. His lungs drew little air into his body; his chest rose and fell almost imperceptibly.

He listened to the early air, searching for some sound to root him in the world. Bird songs circled away through the woods and back again. A dog barked once. A man called out and another, nearby, answered. A footstep brushed the dirt close to Magin, and looking up he saw the woman's face in the doorway.

"Ning," she said, smiling.

Magin tried to raise himself from the bed, but had no strength in his arms.

"Oh no. No, no, no," the woman cried in English with a look of horror on her face, throwing back her head.

"Listen to me," said Magin.

The woman took a breath and rushed on.

"No: tk. Uurk, uursh."

Magin turned away from her. His pain deafened him.

The woman hobbled quickly to the door and called out: "Ruckuck. Tk! No, no!" Magin heard the sound of people coming: a soft rustling and then the ground shaking outside his door.

The people crowded into the hut, filling it with the smell of burning wood and tobacco.

"Tk. Pshsht uuril," said one man, softly.

Magin shrank from the crowd above him.

"Ning," said the woman.

"No, tk, no pshtu tori," said another man, bending over Magin and breathing on his face.

As each minute passed, Magin felt the need for silence more desperately, and his fear grew. He wanted to be alone, to think of Mary, to breathe, and to sleep.

There was almost no air left in the room. Magin's eyesight grew dim. With difficulty, he searched the faces above him for the white-haired old man and did not find him. The woman was smiling in a friendly way. He tried to lift his arm. It was too heavy. Fixing her with his eyes, he said in Trsk, "Bring me water."

She did not understand, and stopped smiling.

A black-bearded man, standing near the bed, puffed on his pipe in quiet contemplation of Magin. Magin hardly breathed. His throat was dry and he could not swallow.

"Water," he said again, hoarsely.

"Water," answered several voices.

Then the black-bearded man said a few guttural words and the people began talking vigorously. "Uurk," said a small man. "No, tsatet ruck!" shouted another. The dogs, who had come to the hut at the heels of the men, became excited and barked sharply, one after another, outside the door. Magin fainted.

When he regained consciousness the room was empty. He tried to think clearly, but his thoughts faded and slipped from his grasp. The pain had wrapped around him tightly. His throat burned. He looked across at the inner wall and followed the grain of the wood. It was dark and water-stained. He looked at the floor. Clumps of snow lay over the pocked dirt. His eyes turned up toward the ceiling, and found only deepening darkness over the beam. His eyes moved down over the outer wall, from stone to stone, until they fixed on the window. There, beyond the pane, was a crowd of faces, staring intently at him.

Startled, he turned away. He heard fingers moving over the sill. Snow rustled below the window. He tried to close his hands around the mattress, testing his strength, and waited for the voices to rise again.

AWAY FROM HOME

It has been so long since she used a metaphor!

COMPANY

I like the students. I like their company. I like them here—
if only they would remain in the indefinite future. They
must be somewhere in my future or they will not be here for
me, for company, where I can talk to them sometimes all
day long. But that future must never come. Because it is so
hard to meet them in the class itself. The problem is that in
order to have the company of them here, in my imagination,
I must pay the price of that future arriving, as it does, with
all the difficulty of that encounter.

Then there is another sort of company in the letters I
have not answered. If I answer the letters, those patient or
impatient people waiting for answers are no longer present
to me. If I answer the letters, I suppose I may be in some
cases present to them, then. But, though not telling myself
this is the reason, I don't answer these letters. And yet this
is selfish, and of course impolite. I answer some, in fact. But
most go unanswered for weeks, months, more than a year,
several years, or forever. Several times, I have waited so long
to answer a letter that the person has moved away. Once,

I waited so long to answer a postcard that my friend died.

But maybe these people are no longer waiting for answers by now anyway; maybe their attention is no longer on me, and this company is only an illusion: the friendly or neutral words are still there on various sheets of paper in different envelopes, but in the minds of these people who wrote the unanswered letters the words for what they are thinking about me, if they think of me at all, are no longer friendly or neutral but unfriendly, dismissive, even disgusted. I believe I have this company, but I do not have it, unless believing this is enough, and I do in some form have this company, whatever they may be thinking.

When I answer one of these letters, true, sometimes all I receive in return, weeks later, is a brief, tired reply. But more often the reply comes quickly and is full, warm, even delighted; and then, just because it is so generous and such wonderful company, it may sit again on my bedside, or on my desk, or on my pile of correspondence, for weeks or months or longer before I answer it.

FINANCES

If they try to add and subtract to see whether the relationship is equal, it won't work. On his side, he is giving
$50,000, she says. No, $70,000, he says. It doesn't matter,
she says. It matters to me, he says. What she is giving is a
half-grown child. Is that an asset or a liability? Now, is she
supposed to feel grateful to him? She can feel grateful, but
not indebted, not that she owes him something. There has
to be a sense of equality. I just love to be with you, she says,
and you love to be with me. I'm grateful to you for provid-
ing for us, and I know my child is sometimes a trouble to
you, though you say he is a good child. But I don't know
how to figure it. If I give all I have and you give all you
have, isn't that a kind of equality? No, he says.

THE TRANSFORMATION

It was not possible, and yet it happened; and not suddenly, but very slowly, not a miracle, but a very natural thing, though it was impossible. A girl in our town turned into a stone. But it is true that she had not been the usual sort of girl even before that: she had been a tree. Now a tree moves in the wind. But sometime near the end of September she began not to move in the wind anymore. For weeks she moved less and less. Then she never moved. When her leaves fell they fell suddenly and with a terrible noise. They crashed onto the cobblestones and sometimes broke into fragments and sometimes remained whole. There would be a spark where they fell and a little white powder lying beside them. People, though I did not, collected her leaves and put them on the mantlepiece. There never was such a town, with stone leaves on every mantlepiece. Then she began to turn gray: at first we thought it was the light. With wrinkled foreheads, twenty of us at a time would stand in a circle around her shading our eyes, dropping our jaws—and so few teeth we had among us it was something to see—and say it was the time of day or the changing season that made her look gray. But soon it was clear that she was simply gray now, just that, the way years ago we had to admit that she was simply a tree now, and no longer a girl. But a tree is one thing and a stone is another. There are limits to what you can accept, even of impossible things.

TWO SISTERS (II)

1

The younger sister is bored in the shop and rings the bell. The older sister comes slowly down the stairs and asks the younger sister why she rang the bell.

The reason is simple: to see her come down. Because she is so fat and moves so slowly; the stairs buckle and creak under her, she has trouble breathing, she holds the banister as if it were still her father's hand, her plump knees knock against each other. It is very amusing to the younger sister and breaks the tedium of the morning.

She says none of this out loud. Out loud she says, "There has been a mistake in yesterday's figures." But of course the older sister cannot find the mistake, though she goes over the figures many times. Her dress is tight under her arms and her ankles are swollen from standing so long.

The younger sister cannot play this trick very often, or she would be found out. But that makes it all the more exciting to her.

2

The two sisters, no longer young, are forced to sleep in the same bed. They dream of different things and carefully hide their dreams from each other in the morning. Sometimes they touch by accident in the bed and fly apart as though they had been burned. They do not sleep well and are not refreshed in the morning. One wakes early, goes to the toilet, and would like to resume sleeping. But there is no joy in going back to bed when her sister lies there already sweating like a sow in the early heat.

3

My sister with thighs like pillars. She eats her potatoes as though she would make a revolution among them, as though they were the People. No, then what is this passion of hers? It is terrifying to see her cloudy eyes become sharp when my dinner is put on the table. I am afraid she will devour not only the dinner but me and my poor life too. Beside her laughter, mine is like the cheeping of a bird in the ivy. No, she never laughs. I never laugh. Her silence, though, is so much greater than mine that mine is like a wisp of smoke in a raincloud.

4

One day the younger sister smacked the older sister in the face. She did it out of frustration and boredom with her life. She regretted it immediately. Not because she had hurt her sister, who stood paralyzed, her hand to her cheek and her hat rolling over the floor, but because now her sister would weep and moan and speak of the incident for months, to the younger sister's shame and anger. She had wanted to diminish her sister in some way, even destroy her, but instead she had given her new dignity.

5

Two sisters, like stone, who do not speak to one another. They have nothing in common but their parentage. One rises early and the other late; one will not eat animal products and the other will not eat whole grains; one has a rash in the summertime and the other cannot wear wool; one will not go to the movies for fear of strange men and the other will not watch television; in every election their votes cancel one another, and they are as no one. Only in their mutual distrust are they alike.

THE FURNACE

My father has trouble with his hearing and does not like to talk on the phone, so I talk on the phone mainly to my mother. Sometimes she abruptly stops what she is saying to me, I hear a noise in the background, she says my name, and waits. Then I know my father has come into the room during her conversation and asked who she is talking to. Sometimes, at that point, he interjects a question for me, but often he asks her something that has nothing to do with me, while I wait at the other end of the phone. After she and I have gone on talking, he may come into the room again, having thought of something else he wants to say. When I hear his voice in the background I stop whatever I am saying to my mother and wait.

Sometimes she forces him to get on the phone. "Tell her yourself," she says. He gets on the phone and without saying hello tells me what it is he wants me to know and then gets off without saying goodbye. Back on the phone, she says, "He's gone."

Although he has never liked to talk on the phone, he has

always liked to write letters. He usually prefers to write a letter that includes some kind of instruction, or at least a transmission of what he thinks will be new information. For a while, we carried on a correspondence whose regularity was unusual for my family, in which very little has ever been regular or systematic. Then I didn't hear from him for some weeks. Maybe I was the one who did not answer his last letter. I told my mother to tell him I would like to hear from him, and he then sent me some clippings from the Crime Beat section of their local paper. In the top margin he had written: "The underside of Cambridge life." Some entries he had marked with a dark line of ink down the side margin.

"...A Jefferson Park man entered the dispute, slashing the teen just below the right eye with an unidentified weapon. While this happened, the Jackson Circle man stole the bike. Later, police found a Jackson Street man riding the bike. Police arrested the Jackson Circle man, Jackson Street man and Jefferson Park man and charged them with assault with a dangerous weapon (knife) and armed robbery."

On another clipping he had underlined certain sentences:

"Police officers recovered two martial arts swords and a meat cleaver."

"At 10 pm an employee of the Cantab Lounge reported that a suspect who had been shut off at the bar assaulted her by throwing a glass at her."

"A Cambridge resident reported that he was assaulted with a fingernail clipper by a suspect who was throwing trash around the doorway at Eddy's Place."

"A Rindge Avenue resident reported that her daughter

hit her over the head with a glass."

"A Rindge Avenue resident reported that she was assaulted with a large pin by two other neighborhood residents."

In the top margin of this clipping he had written:
"Strange weapons dept."

After this he sent me an article he had written. He occasionally wrote an article or a letter to a newspaper about
something that had come up in connection with the Bible
or some other religious topic. The articles and letters were
clever, and by now I was interested in the Bible and religious topics myself.

This one, on circumcision, was called "The Unkindest
Cut" and opened with a sentence about the "male organ." In
his thin, shaky handwriting, he had noted in the margin at
the top of the article that I shouldn't feel I had to read this,
nor should my husband feel he had to read it. He was sincere, but he often attached disclaimers to the articles and
letters he sent and I generally disregarded them.

Yet when I tried to read the article, I found it hard to
read so much about the male organ as written by my father.
I asked my husband if he would read it and tell me the gist
of it but he did not really want to read it either. I did not
know what to do about this situation, since it would have
been awkward even to mention it to my father, but in time,
as I took no action, I began to forget it. My father had probably forgotten it long before, since his memory has become
more and more undependable, as he and my mother both
point out.

But the letters he was sending me for a while were about
the household he grew up in: besides his mother and father,

there were two grandmothers and a grandfather who was slightly mad, maids, cooks, and cleaning women who came and went, and his grandmothers' female nurse-companions and his grandfather's male nurse-companions, who also came and went. His father's mother owned the house and dominated it, to his mother's annoyance. I have seen this house, which still stands in a street not far from where they live, and it looks to me surprisingly modest to have held such a number and variety of people. The last time it was sold, he read about the sale in the paper and wrote to the new owners, explaining that he had been born in the upstairs front room and had played in the hayloft of the small barn. The new owners were pleased to hear from him and sent him photographs of the house.

He would write to me in some detail and in the midst of it apologize, saying that what lay immediately ahead would be tedious and that I could read fast or skim if I liked. He said he was trying to recover facts that he had not thought of for most of a century. But I would write back asking for even more detail, because I wanted to come as close as I could to a way of life that seemed to me precious for several reasons, one being simply that even the memory of it was slipping away, because fewer and fewer people were alive who had experienced it.

Most recently we had gotten into a correspondence about the furnace in the house where he grew up. He said that while he lived there, changes had occurred, but they were all additions, and what was there to begin with remained. For instance, a gas stove was installed in the kitchen alongside the coal stove. His grandmother felt that for certain things the coal stove was more economical. A new oil furnace was added in the basement, but the huge old coal furnace remained. At some point electricity was added to gas for lighting. His grandmother kept both because in a storm, she warned them, the electricity might fail.

He remembered how one of the cleaning women used to comb her long hair in the kitchen at the end of the day, so that she could go forth suitably neat. She would then extract the hairs from the comb and put them, not in the stove, which required the effort of lifting one of the iron covers, but on top of the stove, where they burned to an ash that remained visible until someone thought to remove it.

In the early days, he said, a "furnace man" would come at about seven in the morning to shake down the big furnace, remove ashes and clinkers, and shovel more coal in from one of the two big bins whose board sides projected into the cellar, resting on the cellar floor. An early furnace man was named Frank and his grandmother continued to call subsequent ones "Frank" as her memory for names weakened. The furnace was a matter of constant concern in very cold weather. Even when his father was home, his grandmother would go down to investigate, and then, in order to force his father to act, would do something deliberately noisy to it. He would shout "Mother, Mother," pounding on the floor with his foot, and rush down the cellar stairs. She was not supposed to go down them, for they had no banisters, and there was a drop on either side to the cellar floor below. The only lighting came from the open door of the kitchen, from tiny dirty outdoor windows at ground level, and from a gas pipe that came down from the ceiling and supplied the same kind of feeble, naked flame that his mother used in her room to heat her curling iron.

On ash collection days the furnace man lifted the barrels up the steps of the bulkhead. In winter, a boardwalk was put down from the street in front to the bulkhead. Along this, or in the soft gravel when the walk was not in place, the furnace-man, on the days of the city collection, rotated the tilted ash barrels. To bring the coal in, along the same boardwalk, required a two-man team: one man would shovel the coal into a container on the back of the second man, who would carry it into the yard, unshoulder it with a twist of his body, and dump it down the chute. Coal delivery was by horse and wagon when my father was a child. He said on a normal working day there would be at least three horses and wagons on his street, delivering ice, coal, milk, groceries, fruits and vegetables, or express packages, or peddling, or buying old newspapers or old iron. There was also a horse-drawn hurdy-gurdy.

What he said about his furnace and all the trappings of the furnace made me go down and look more carefully at our own furnace. Our house is either a hundred years old or a hundred and fifty, depending on which town historical document we believe. This furnace was converted to gas from coal probably forty years ago. The trappings were still there, a coal hod on the floor of the coal bin and, hanging on the wall, pronged iron bars for opening the hatches. I looked up and saw two long, stout boards stowed above the coal bin. Now that I had read what my father wrote about the men bringing the coal in across the snow, I had no doubt these boards were put down for the coal delivery here too. I was excited to discover this.

I wrote back to my father about what I had discovered, knowing that for several reasons he would be less interested in my coal furnace than his memories of his own. It is natural for an old man to be engrossed in his memories and less interested in the present. But he has always been more interested in his own ideas than anyone else's.

Although he likes to have conversations with other people and hear what they say, he does not know what to do with an idea of someone else's except to use it as a starting point from which to produce an even better idea of his own. His own ideas are certainly interesting, often the most interesting in a given situation. He has always been interesting at a dinner party, even though as he aged, a time came when he would have to leave the table part of the way through and go lie down for a while.

Dinner parties were an important part of the life my mother and father had together from the very beginning. There was a skill to taking part in a dinner party, and a technique to giving one, especially to guiding the conversation at the table. There was an art to encouraging a shy guest, or subduing a noisy one. My mother and father are still sociable, but they are handicapped by their age now and limit what they do. Now they have people in for tea more often than dinner, and at a certain point during the tea, also, my father leaves the room to go lie down.

Though my mother still goes out to concerts and lectures, my father rarely does. One of the last events they went to together was a grand birthday party held in a public library. Four hundred guests were invited, coming from around the world. My mother told me about it, including the fact that during the party my father fell down. He was not hurt. She was not in the same room with him when he fell.

He is unsteady on his feet, and has fallen or come close to falling quite often in the last few years. I was present when a health technician came to give advice about rearranging the apartment so that it would be safer for the two of them. The health technician observed my father there in the apartment for a while. My father's head is large and heavy and his body is thin and frail. The technician said he noticed that my father tended to toss his head back, and this threw him off balance. The technician said he should try to change that habit and also use his walker in the house. Although the technician was friendly and helpful, he was very energetic and spoke in a loud voice, and toward the end of the visit my father became too agitated to stay in his company any longer and left to go lie down. After that visit, my mother told me, my father tried to remember to use his walker but tended to leave it here and there in the apartment and then had to walk around without it to find it again.

If I ask my mother, on the telephone, how my father is, she often lowers her voice to answer. She often says she is worried about him. She has been worried for years. She is always worried about some recent or new behavior of his. She does not seem to realize that this behavior is not always recent or new, or that she is always worried about something. Sometimes she is worried because he is depressed. For a while she was worried because he so often became hysterically angry. Not long ago she said he seemed to take an unnatural interest in their Scrabble games. After that she said he was losing his memory, did not remember incidents from their life together, kept referring to one family member by the name of another, and sometimes did not recognize a name at all.

He had to stay in a rehabilitation hospital for a while after his last fall, to have some physical therapy. To my mother's astonishment, he did not mind playing catch with the other patients in the physical therapy group, or tossing a beanbag in a contest. She said this was not like him: she wondered if he was regressing to a childish state. She suspected that he had enjoyed the attention there, and the food. Since his return home, she told me, he had not been eating very well. She was upset because he did not seem to like her cooking anymore. On the other hand he did finish a piece of writing he was working on.

A year ago, when my mother herself was in the hospital with a serious illness, he and I went out to look for a restaurant where we could have supper before going back to sit with my mother. It was a cold, windy night in May. We were downtown in the city, in a neighborhood of hospitals, tall well-lighted buildings all around us. There were walkways over our heads, and underground garages opening on all sides, but no restaurants that I could see. Stores were closed, not many cars went by on the streets and almost no people walked on the sidewalk. My father was unsteady on his feet and I was watching for every curb and uneven piece of pavement. He was determined to find a restaurant where he could have an alcoholic drink. At last, we entered a passageway in one of the tall buildings, walking into what looked from the outside to be a deserted mall. Going down an empty corridor and past some empty store windows and up some steps, we found a restaurant with a bar and an amount of good cheer and number of lively customers surprising after the empty streets outside. We sat down at a table and talked a little, but my father's mind was on his drink and he kept looking for the waiter, who was too busy to come to our table. I was thinking that this dinner was likely to be the last one I would have in a restaurant with my father, and certainly the least festive.

In an upper floor of one of the tall buildings nearby, my mother lay suffering from a rare blood disorder and all the other ills that came one after another because of the treatment itself. We thought she might be dying, though my father seemed to forget this at times, or rather, if she seemed better one day, he cheered up completely and began making jokes again, as though she would certainly get well. The next day he might arrive at the hospital to find one of us crying and his face would fall.

My father grew so impatient for his drink that he stood up on his unsteady legs, bracing himself with his cane. The waiter came. My father ordered his drink. What he wanted so much was a Perfect Rob Roy.

His hearing is not good, and his eyesight is not very good either, and for a while, if I asked him how he was, he would say that except for his eyes and his ears, his balance, his memory, and his teeth, he was doing reasonably well. In order to read certain sizes of print he has to take off his glasses and hold the text within an inch or two of his nose. It used to be that sometimes, when I asked my mother how my father was, she would answer: "He was well enough to go to the Theological Library today." Then he stopped going to any library because it was so hard for him to see the titles of the books and to bend down to the lower shelves. Then his balance became so bad it was very risky for him to go out by himself at all. Once he fell in the street and hit the back of his head. A stranger passing in a car called an ambulance on his cell phone. It was after that fall that he went into the hospital for physical therapy and after he returned home did not go out by himself anymore. On one of my last visits, at Christmas, he said he needed a magnifying light for the large dictionary in the living room.

He has always enjoyed looking things up in the dictionary, particularly word histories. Now my mother says she is worried about him because he is no longer merely interested in word histories but obsessed by them. He will get up from a conversation with a guest at tea and go look up a word she has used. He will interrupt the conversation to report the etymology. He has always preferred an illustrated dictionary. He likes to study the pictures, particularly the pictures of handsome women. At Christmas, he showed me one of his favorites, the President of Iceland.

I have gone down to look at the furnace again because in a few days it will be removed and new one put in its place. The dust is deep and gray in the old coal bin. The wooden planks that form the sides are rich in color and smoothly fitted together. Tossed in the dust and half buried are the old coal hod and some metal parts of the coal chute. I ask my husband if the men who come to install the new furnace will have to remove the walls of the coal bin and he says he thinks they will not.

After I wrote to my father about my discovery of the boards, he answered my letter with another about his childhood and also another memory of coal men, this one dating from when he was grown up. He said he was out driving with my sister next to him in the car when he happened upon an accident that had just occurred. He said that two men had been delivering coal. The delivery truck had been parked at an angle in a driveway. The driver was talking to the owner of the house, presumably about the delivery. The second man, his assistant, was standing at the end of the driveway with his back to the truck, looking out at the street. The truck's brakes were apparently faulty and the truck rolled backward down the driveway. Either no one saw this or no one cried out in time, the coal man's assistant was struck by the truck and run over, and his head was crushed. My father said he drove some distance past the accident, parked his car and, instructing my sister to stay where she was, went back to look. A short way beyond the man's crushed head, he saw the man's brains on the pavement.

My father said he knew he was wrong to go and look, he should have driven on. Then he began to talk about the anatomy of the brain, that the incident dramatized a conviction he had always had. He had always believed that consciousness was so dependent on the physical brain that the continuation of consciousness and one's identity after death was inconceivable. He admitted that this conviction was probably metaphysically naive, but added that it had been strengthened by a lifetime's observation of many insane and manic-depressive types, some in his own family. Among the manic-depressive types, he said, he included himself. Then he went on to talk about the mind of God, whom he described as a Being with presumably no neurones.

Now the new furnace is installed and working but the house does not seem any warmer. The rooms that were always chilly before are still chilly. There is still a perceptible change in temperature as we go up to the second floor. The only difference is that because this new furnace works with fans, we can hear it while it is on. It is much smaller than the old one, and shiny. It makes a better impression on anyone visiting the basement, which was one reason to get it, I realize now, since we may one day want to sell this house. I have cleaned out the coal bin, at last, preserving the coal hod and the sections of chute and storing them in another wooden stall in a part of the cellar we haven't touched yet that contains an old pump, among other things.

My correspondence with my father about the furnace seems to have ended, as has our correspondence about his family. His letters, in fact, have shrunk to small scrawled notes attached to more clippings from the local paper.

Twice he has sent my husband and me the same "Ask Marjorie" column, one that discusses the shape of the earth and points out that the ancients knew perfectly well that the earth was round. Both times he wrote a message on the back of the envelope asking my husband and me if we were taught that in ancient times people believed the earth was flat.

He has also sent me more items from the "Crime Beat" section.

"At 10:30 pm a Putnam Avenue resident said an unknown person broke into the home by pushing in the rear door. A dollar bill was taken."

"At 9:12 am a North Cambridge man from Mass. Ave. said someone had broken in but nothing was missing."

"A Belmont resident working at a Mass. Ave. address stated that another employee told her that she had been fired and then proceeded to scratch the victim in the neck." By this one he wrote in the margin: "Why? What is the connection?"

"Friday, March 11. At 11:30 pm, a Concord Avenue woman was walking down Garden Street near Mass. Ave. when a man asked her 'Are you smiling?' The woman said yes, so the man punched her in the mouth, causing her lip to bleed and swell. No arrests were made."

"Three men were arrested for assault and battery on Third Street near Gore Street at 2:50 am. Two men are Cambridge residents, both charged with assault and battery with a dangerous weapon, a shod foot. A Billerica man received the same charge, but with a hammer." My father put an X in the margin beside the grammar mistake.

"Tuesday, June 13. A Rhode Island resident reported that between 8:45 am and 10 am, at an address on Garden St., an unknown person took her purse with $180 and credit cards. A male was witnessed under the table but the victim believed that it was someone from the power company."

On my last visit, my father seemed in worse condition than I had seen him before. When I asked him if he was working on anything in particular now, he said, "No," and then turned his head slowly to my mother and looked at her in bewilderment, his mouth hanging open. There was an expression of pain or agony on his face that seemed habitual. She looked back at him, waited a moment, impassive, and then said: "Yes, you are. You're writing about the Bible and anti-Semitism." He continued to stare at her.

Later that evening, before he went to bed, he said: "This is symptomatic of my condition: You're my daughter, and I'm proud of you, but I have nothing to say to you."

He left to get ready for bed, and then came back into the room wearing dazzling white pajamas. My mother asked me to admire his pajamas, and he stood quietly while I did. Then he said: "I don't know what I will be like in the morning."

After he went to bed, my mother showed me a picture of him forty years before sitting at a seminar table surrounded by students. "Just look at him there!" she said in distress, as though it were some sort of punishment that he had become what he was now—an old man with a beaked profile like a nutcracker.

Saying goodbye, I held his hand longer than usual. He may not have liked it. It is impossible to tell what he is feeling, often, but physical contact has always been difficult for him, and he has always been awkward about it. Whether out of embarrassment or absent-mindedness, he kept shaking his hand and mine up and down slightly, as though palsied.

Recently, my mother said he was still worse. He had fallen again, and he was having trouble with his bladder. Can he still work? I asked her. To me, it seemed that if he could still work, then he was all right, no matter what else was going wrong with him. Not really, she said. "He has been writing letters, but there are odd things in some of them. It may not matter, since they're mostly to old friends." She said maybe she should be checking them, though, before he sent them.

It was a phone conversation with another old woman that reminded me of a name I had forgotten for this time of life. After telling me about her angioplasty and her diabetes, she said. "Well, this is what you can expect when you enter the twilight years." But it is hard not to think that my father's bewilderment is only temporary, and that behind it, his sharp critical mind is still alive and well. With this younger, firmer mind he will continue to read the letters I send him and write back—our correspondence is only temporarily interrupted.

The latest letter I have seen from him was not written to me but to one of his grandsons. My mother thought I should see it before she sent it. The envelope was taped shut with strong packing tape. The entire letter concerns a mathematical rhyme he copied from the newspaper. It begins:

"A dozen, a gross and a score
plus three times the square root of four
divide it by seven plus five times eleven
equals nine to the square and not more."

Then he explains mathematical terms and the solution of this problem. Because he changed the margins of his page to type the poem, and did not reset them, the whole letter is written in short lines like a poem:

"The total to be divided by 7 consists
of the following:
12 plus 144 plus 20 plus 3 times
the square root of 4.
These are the numerals above the line
over the divisor 7. They add up to 182,
which divided by seven equals 26.

26 plus 11 times 5 (55) is 81.
81 is 9 squared. A number squared
is a number multiplied by itself.
The square of 9 is nine times nine or 81."

He goes on to explain the concept of squaring numbers, and of the cube, along the way giving the etymologies of certain words, including *dozen*, *score*, and *scoreboard*. He talks about the sign for square root being related to the form of a tree.

I tell my mother the letter seems a little strange to me. She protests, saying that it is quite correct. I don't argue, but say he can certainly send it. The end of the letter is less strange, except for the line breaks:

"For me memory and balance fail rapidly.
You are young and have a university library
system for your use. I, who have
a good home reference collection,
sometimes can get other people to
look up things for me, but it is not the same.
I have to explain that I have increasingly
lost my memory and sense of balance,
I can't go any where, not the libraries
or the book stores to browse. We have to pay
a young woman to walk out with me
and prevent me from falling
though I take a mechanical walker with me.
I don't mean it has an engine that propels it.
I do the propelling, but that it is
shiny and metal and has wheels."

YOUNG AND POOR

I like working near the baby, here at my desk by lamplight.
The baby sleeps.

As though I were young and poor again, I was going
to say.

But I am still young and poor.

THE SILENCE OF MRS. ILN

Her children found it impossible to understand old Mrs. Iln now. They were forced to call her senile. But if they had paused a moment from their wild activities and tried to imagine her state of mind, they would have known that this was not the case.

Decades before, when her recent marriage had cast a pleasant light over her otherwise homely features, she had been as articulate as any other woman, perhaps even more articulate than was necessary. If her husband asked her where his cufflinks were, she might answer, "I think they are in the top drawer of your bureau, though it could be that you took them off in the dining room and they are still there, on the table, or perhaps they have fallen onto the floor by now, in all this confusion; if they got stepped on I don't know what I would do, I just don't know..." When she had had a little wine and felt moved to give her opinion of the political situation, she would burst out with "You know what I think? I think it's a case of collective madness: I think they're all insane, we're all insane, but it isn't our fault, and it isn't the fault of our parents, and it isn't the fault of our parents' parents. I don't know whose fault it is, but I would like to know..."

A few years later, she and her husband understood one another too well to need long explanations. Her opinions did not change over time, but hardened into obsessive and monotonous responses, and remained thoroughly familiar to her husband. She began to curtail her sentences, and her meaning was always clear to her husband and to her children, as they grew up. When her children left home, one by one, Mrs. Iln was gradually overcome by the feeling that she had no purpose in the world and no reason to be alive. She lost sight of herself completely. Her husband had grown into her until she hardly distinguished him from herself, and now her sentences were reduced to a few words: "Dresser drawer in your bedroom," she would say, or "completely insane." Since her husband knew what she was going to say before she said it, even those few words were unnecessary and in time were left unspoken. "I wonder where my cufflinks are," her husband would say softly, more to himself than to her. And even before she wagged her head toward the bureau, he would be there rummaging among his handkerchiefs and foreign coins. Or when he read aloud to her from the morning paper she would purse her lips and give him a certain stormy look and he would hear the "insane" of a few years before echoing in the air. He too might have stopped speaking, if he had not grown to like the constant murmur from his own lips.

Since nothing happened in her house that had not happened before, since her children, who found her silence unnerving after the din of their own homes, rarely visited her, Mrs. Iln no longer had any reason to speak, and silence became a deeply rooted habit. When her husband fell gravely ill, she tended him silently; when he died, she had no words for her grief; when her oldest children asked her to live with them, she shook her head and went home.

Sometimes she felt the need to give a word or two of explanation especially to her grandchildren, as she watched them from beyond her wall of silence; sometimes her children begged her to speak, as though it would prove something to them. And at these times she struggled as though in a nightmare to bring out one sound, and could not. It was as if by speaking she would have damaged something inside herself.

More and more often in her loneliness, thoughts would come to her as they had never come before, not even in her youth. They were thoughts more complex than "insanity," and she would hear the words mounting in turmoil within her. But when her children came at the weekend to sit with her for an hour or two, it was hard to find the right moment to begin speaking of all she had thought, and if the moment came, when their restless chatter stopped and their eyes fell on her old pitted face, then she could rarely summon the words that had flown hither and thither in her head all week. And if she managed to summon the words to her mind, then she could never, never break through the last barrier and free herself from the constriction of her speechlessness.

At last she stopped trying, and when her children came they saw an expression on her face that had not been there before—a stiff, dead look, a look of blankness and defeat that reflected her hopelessness. They immediately seized upon this expression as evidence of senility. She was astonished and hurt by their reaction. If they had been more patient with her, if they had stayed with her for longer periods of time, they would have seen something in her that was not senility. Yet they clung to the idea of senility and registered her name in a nursing home.

At first she was horrified, and everything in her cried out against the coming change. With renewed vigor she frowned at them and sent them a look that her husband had well understood. But they were not moved. In their eyes, her every gesture could now be called senile. Even quite normal behavior seemed mad to them, and nothing she did could reach them.

But once she was actually living in the nursing home, she made peace with her surroundings. During the day she sat in the library reading and thinking. She read very slowly and spent many more hours staring at the wall than at the book. She tested her mind against what she read and it grew stronger. Only the nurses were not quite real to her and puzzled her: she thought their brittle good humor was not honest. They did not like her, because her lucid eye made them uneasy. But she moved comfortably among her bloodless, wrinkled companions, more comfortably than she had ever moved among the vigorous people of her former life. She found the silence in the crowded dining room appropriate. She understood very well the morose men and women who struggled along the garden paths in the afternoon or sat staring through the porch railings at the street during the

long summer twilight. Tentatively at first, and with growing wonder, she realized that she had been nearly dead
among the living. Among the nearly dead, she was at last
beginning to live.

ALMOST OVER:
SEPARATE BEDROOMS

They have moved into separate bedrooms now.
That night she dreams she is holding him in her arms. He
dreams he is having dinner with Ben Jonson.

MONEY

I don't want any more gifts, cards, phone calls, prizes, clothes, friends, letters, books, souvenirs, pets, magazines, land, machines, houses, entertainments, honors, good news, dinners, jewels, vacations, flowers, or telegrams. I just want money.

ACKNOWLEDGMENT

I have only to add
that the plates in the present volume
have been carefully re-etched
by Mr. Cuff.

13· AUG· 07   Midwest $13.02 ($14.00)   102717